# RUTHLESS BILLIONAIRE

SIERRA CARTWRIGHT

RUTHLESS BILLIONAIRE

First E-book Publication: March 2022

Line Editing by GG Royale

Proofing by Bev Albin and Cassie Hess-Dean

Layout Design by Once Upon An Alpha

Cover Design by Rachel Connolly, PA

Photo provided by Wander Aguiar

Model: Rodiney Santiago

Promotion by Once Upon An Alpha, Shannon Hunt

Adult Reading Material

Disclaimer: This work of fiction is for mature (18+) audiences only and contains strong sexual content and situations.

It is a standalone with my guarantee of satisfying happily ever after.

*For late nights, early mornings, and all the coffee. For everyone whose support keeps me going. I appreciate you. Special shout-outs this time to Bev, GG, Cassie, Shannon, Shayla, Amy, Linda, Whit. Thank you!*

# PROLOGUE

"I can't believe we're doing this."

Lucas Rutherford grinned at his younger sister as they strode across the pier leading to a makeshift tent in front of *Stargazer*, the luxury yacht docked in Galveston, Texas. "Should be...interesting." Much better to spend New Year's Eve among friends than all alone, watching the clock, counting his regrets, like he had the last two years.

The moment he and Lyla neared the entrance, a smiling hostess greeted them. "Good afternoon, sir."

Off to the side stood a serious-looking woman wearing a windbreaker emblazoned with a Hawkeye Security patch. Despite the fact she was petite, Lucas had no doubt she could kick his ass from one side of the Gulf of Mexico to the other.

Lucas fished the invite—it was hand lettered and actually arrived in the mail—from the pocket of his blazer. "Lucas Rutherford. My plus-one is my sister, Lyla."

The hostess scanned for his name on an electronic pad. "We're glad to have you. Enjoy your evening." With a practiced, professional smile, she indicated they could continue on.

"Fancy," Lyla said.

Which he'd expected.

Lucas's friend, Rafe Sterling, had rented the craft for a New Year's Eve celebration with some of his closest friends. Because he was in the hospitality industry, owner of some of the world's most renowned properties, he never did anything by half measures.

They strode up the gangplank toward the boat...if that was the correct term for something this enormous.

Once they were aboard, the captain greeted them by name. No doubt the hostess had radioed ahead, but it was still a nice touch.

Within moments, they had champagne flutes in hand.

For the last day in December, the day was unseasonably warm, in the low seventies, with a light southerly breeze. Perfect for the cruise into Galveston Bay and up to Kemah for the midnight firework display.

"I was so ready for this."

By unspoken accord, he and his little sister walked to the railing. The early winter sunshine cast its rays on the water, making it shimmer and glisten.

Lyla sighed. "For someone who lives here, I don't spend enough time on the water."

His only sibling was a painter whose efforts had been dismissed—and worse, discouraged—by their parents. When she received the first part of her inheritance, she'd started an artists' community on the island. Each year, she offered several residencies that included studio space, a one-bedroom apartment, along with a small stipend to others whose talent needed a place to thrive. Running it consumed her.

Ironic, he mused.

In an effort to find the freedom to pursue her dreams and

set her own schedule, she put in at least as many hours as Lucas and their father. "You work too hard."

Feathering back her hair, she turned to him. "Hello? Are you listening to yourself?"

He grimaced.

"When was your last vacation?"

Damned if he could remember.

"Your honeymoon? I mean, the first one. You didn't go on one after the second marriage if I recall."

*Fuck.* His little sister knew where all of his vulnerabilities were buried. Just like when they'd been kids, she wasn't afraid to poke at them. "Going for the jugular today?"

Rather than pursuing the conversation further, he sipped from his glass. Delighted by the explosion of citrus acidity on his tongue, he raised an eyebrow. Whiskey was his poison of choice, but for bubbly, this stuff wasn't bad.

"I'm being serious."

Had he really expected that she'd give up and move on? "Like you, I have a business to build." Also like her, he planned to avoid joining the family business for as many years as possible.

"Idle hands are the devil's workshop." Lyla parroted their mother's oft-repeated mantra.

Maybe he'd heard it so much that he actually believed it.

"This reminds me there's more to life."

"Especially for an artist. You need the inspiration."

"We all need to get away and clear our minds. I think we'd be sharper." She took a sip from her glass. "Maybe happier."

Whatever that meant. Responsibility came before anything. He was expected to honor his parents and the obligations that came along with being among the first families to settle in Texas. Many of their forebearers had served in the state legislature, and service to the community was an expectation.

"Mom told me Dad's blood pressure is still high. Medication isn't controlling it as they hoped it would."

Lucas exhaled. Because he was always at the helm of Rutherford Enterprises, Lawrence didn't take care of himself. If he slept five hours a night, he called himself lazy. When he bothered to eat at all, he paid no attention to what he consumed. Exercise was for those with extra time.

"I thought I'd give you a fair warning. When we get together with them tomorrow, they want to talk to you about taking a larger role in the company."

*No chance.* To avoid his instinctive answer, he took a second drink.

"Which means they want you to get married." She grinned. "Again."

Which was part of the truth. They expected him to produce an heir and a spare—and they needed to be legitimate to avoid being thrust into an unsavory spotlight. His parents had done their part to continue the lineage. Now it was up to him. He wouldn't allow the Rutherford name to end as a footnote in some history book. Or rather as a forgotten notation on the internet. Perish the thought.

"I'm not looking forward to it. Not that I ever do."

New Year's Day at the family's River Oaks estate in Houston was a time-honored tradition that had to be preserved. His mother cooked black-eyed peas, or so she claimed, for good luck. But since it was the only command performance each year, both he and Lyla attended. And they grabbed a drink together afterward. *That* was the biggest reason he showed up.

"Thanks for letting me tag along. This was a surprise."

It had been to him as well.

When he'd seen Rafe at a recent holiday party, he'd mentioned he had a business prospect to discuss. The next morning the invitation had arrived. No doubt there was a correlation. Chartering the *Stargazer* was clearly not an inexpensive proposition, so whatever Rafe had going on had to be big. And Lucas was intrigued.

Further conversation was prevented by the arrival of Hope Malone, Rafe's beautiful fiancée, and unfortunately for him, a professional matchmaker who'd made it clear she'd welcome him as a client.

"Happy New Year!" She lifted onto her tiptoes to kiss his cheek.

"Hope. Beautiful as always."

"And you are a silver-tongued devil." She smiled. Then she looked at his sister. "You must be Lyla. I'm Hope Malone. We're so glad you could join us."

"Thanks for the invite." As she laughed a little, Lyla shook Hope's hand. "Well, not that you did actually. I'm just tagging along since my brother has no one else who'll go anywhere with him."

Hope grinned. "I'm hoping to remedy that."

"Moving on." Lucas shook his head.

"How's that?" Obviously interested, Lyla leaned forward.

"Hope is a matchmaker."

"Seriously?"

"We specialize in finding the perfect person for even the most discerning individual."

"Oh. Never mind. For a minute there, I had some hope. But my brother's not your ideal client."

In warning, he growled at his little sister.

Undaunted, she went on. "Clearly he's not discerning enough about the women he chooses."

He winced as her barb found its mark.

"I like you already, Lyla." Hope laughed. "At any rate, I'm delighted to finally meet you. Your portfolio is inspiring, Ms. Rutherford."

Lyla gave Hope a wide-eyed stare. "You looked me up?"

"Absolutely. And I'll admit, there's a work I'm interested in buying."

"Are you...?" Lyla looked at Lucas as if to see if he arranged this.

He lifted a shoulder. "I haven't said a word about who you are or your extraordinary talent."

"I like to know something about all of our guests, so I did a little research before you arrived. If it's still for sale, I'm interested in purchasing *Soul Searching*."

Her knowledge and enthusiasm impressed Lucas. Though his sister did well, her works were not for everyone. One critic had called them dark, filled with slashes of bold color choices that evoked emotion. Because Lucas was probably one of the closest people to her, he knew they represented the angst she'd buried deep inside her psyche.

"A print?"

"The original, of course. Assuming it's available."

Evidently rendered speechless, Lyla just nodded.

"I'll be in touch soon," Hope promised. "If you'll excuse me, I see that Braden and Elizabeth have arrived. You can find Rafe inside the rear cockpit lounge whenever you're ready."

Evidently sensing his confusion, she clarified her comment. "It's on this deck."

They said a quick goodbye, and moments later Lyla shook her head. "Did that really happen? Or am I dreaming?"

"You've sold a lot of paintings over the years."

"But not to someone like Hope."

He knew what Lyla meant. A woman of great influence. A Titan. Hope had recently been inducted into the Zetas, a secret society. Every generation of the Rutherfords had belonged, almost from the beginning in the 1800s. Though Lyla was eligible for membership because of their family's legacy support of the organization, she hadn't pursued the opportunity. "Not everyone who belongs is a stuffy old person who wants to run the world that they're totally out of touch with."

While he grinned, she groaned. As she should, Lyla recognized the words. She uttered them often enough, mostly to annoy their parents, he surmised.

"This could really be a boost to my career."

One she should have been enjoying for years. "And maybe allow you to do more fundraising."

"I'd rather talk about your marriage prospects."

Or lack of them. Although he hadn't followed up with Hope when she'd pitched her services to him, he had to admit he wasn't doing much better by himself.

"When was the last time you went on a date?"

Rather than answer, he placed his empty glass on the tray of a passing server. "We should say hello to Rafe."

They found Rafe and the rest of the guests who'd already arrived in the lounge, as promised.

Appetizers were arranged on a table, and a bartender was on duty.

The space, as with everything else on the yacht, was spectacular. All furnishings were high end, stainless steel was polished to a bright glow, chandeliers splashed bright welcoming light everywhere, and after four, Lucas lost count of the variety of stone he counted.

When Rafe saw them, he excused himself and made his way over. Instead of saying hello to Lucas, Rafe greeted Lyla with the same enthusiasm his soon-to-be wife had shown.

"Do you have a card?"

She shook her head. "I wasn't planning to do any work while I was here."

"In that case, be sure to get our contact information from Lucas."

Lucas's response was dry. "Didn't know if you realized I was here."

"Hello, Lucas." Rafe responded in a similar deadpan manner. "Been here long?"

The two shook hands and exchanged good-natured banter. "Nice boat." Maybe the largest pleasure vessel ever docked in Galveston, according to Lyla.

"Turns out the owner has bought himself another yacht. He outgrew this one."

"I see." Lucas didn't know how else to respond. How did someone outgrow a boat this size?

"He wants to keep it but offload some of the expense."

"Seems prudent." Keeping the crew employed had to cost a fortune. Not that he didn't know plenty of people who could afford it. Lucas just tended to be much more risk averse. He preferred to make money than to spend it. And he made a living capitalizing on others' poor fiscal decisions.

"Elizabeth suggested we add it to our amenities."

Elizabeth Ryan was his friend Braden's fiancée, and Rafe's VP of Premier Concierge Services. She catered to the most elite members of his chain's rewards program by arranging for experiences all over the world. From islands with a master chef and massage therapy experiences, to Antarctic treks.

"I wasn't sure about it, so she convinced the owner to let us enjoy the experience for ourselves."

"Win all around." Lucas grinned. It was exactly the kind of deal he would have made, so he appreciated Elizabeth's strategic move.

Lyla accepted another glass of bubbly. "I'm a fortunate recipient of her brilliance."

Lucas glanced around. He recognized every person in the room. Some of them had hired him to turnaround their businesses. A quick calculation of net worth was over a hundred billion dollars. "Going to give any hints why you've gathered us all here?"

Rafe shrugged. "Fireworks over the water are always an exceptional way to welcome a New Year."

If there was a more tightlipped person, Lucas hadn't met him. No doubt the evening would be memorable.

"Help yourselves to food, but don't fill up too much. We're having dinner at seven in the dining room." Rafe moved off to visit with other friends.

Which left a few hours to enjoy the venue—a movie in the media room, conversation in the lounge or outside, a tour of the bridge, games on one deck, the swimming pool on another. As for Lucas, it wasn't nearly warm enough for him to consider stripping off his clothes and jumping in.

They chatted with a few people, and then Elizabeth and Braden joined them on the back deck.

Soon Lyla was chatting about the artist community, and Elizabeth's eyes lit up. "That's the exact kind of experience our Premier members would love."

"Seriously?"

"Are you interested in expanding the program?"

Mouth open, Lyla looked at Lucas. He shrugged. He was glad she'd come with him.

"Will you excuse us?" Elizabeth asked before the two ladies moved to one side of the lounge.

Braden watched his bride-to-be walk away.

"You have any idea why Rafe invited us all? Besides trying out the *Stargazer*?"

"Second-round fundraising."

He was intrigued. "For...?"

"A top-secret project. The person would like to remain anonymous for now."

Lucas had a guess, however. It had to be someone

everyone knew. Or had at least heard of. Only a few names came to mind.

"We'll be discussing it after dinner."

Lucas nodded. Braden was no fool. Of course the big reveal would be after everyone had socialized, eaten, and had been loosened up by a couple of drinks.

From the far side of the room, Elizabeth looked over at Braden. Their gazes met, and they both smiled. Elizabeth flushed scarlet before returning her attention to Lyla.

How the mighty had fallen. At one point Braden's name had regularly appeared on gossip sites. He'd been referred to the "Scandalous Billionaire" for his numerous affairs. Until his housekeeper's daughter had brought him to his knees.

With a smoothness Lucas didn't expect, *Stargazer* departed from the pier.

For the next hour, while Lyla joined a group who'd gathered to watch the latest blockbuster film, Lucas caught up with other friends and discussed far too much business, even though it was interspersed with talk of college and professional football. Jaxon Mills and his new wife, Willow, had box seats for the Super Bowl and invited Lucas to join them. "You can bring a date."

Except he couldn't because he didn't have a girlfriend. Maybe he could bring Rykker, a friend with no more prospects than Lucas had. Barring that, maybe Zane Kentwood. He too was a member of the Works too Much and Sucks at Love Club.

"Hey, Lucas," Jaxon shouted from the back of the lounge. "I need a partner for cornhole. On the aft deck. Can't let the judge and Elizabeth beat us."

Though he'd never played the game, the challenge sparked his competitive instincts.

He joined the small group outside and familiarized himself with the few rules of the beanbag-toss game. Then he took a couple of practice shots. After all, winning was more important than anything.

When the sun set and the air on the open water turned a little chillier, the judge suggested they stop the game. Naturally since he and Elizabeth were up by a point.

Lucas shook his head. "Only if get a rematch at a later date."

"Ah hell no." The judge grinned.

Laughing, they meandered back inside.

An hour and a half later, Hope made her rounds to invite them to be seated for dinner.

His watch said it was precisely the top of the hour when servers presented menus to each person and filled one of two waiting glasses with a dry white wine.

Across the table, Lyla met his gaze. Whatever was going on was going to be interesting.

But even if he'd been placing bets, he wouldn't have put money on the fact that a helicopter would land on the back of the *Stargazer*.

And he sure as hell wouldn't have guessed who would emerge from beneath the rotors.

# CHAPTER ONE

Damn, he was gorgeous. No matter how hard she tried, Wynter couldn't look away from the picture she was staring at on her phone. None other than asshole billionaire Lucas Rutherford.

His gray eyes were stormy, and a reflection made it appear as if bolts of lightning were striking in their depths. He didn't smile for the headshot, and in fact his features radiated the impatience he was known for, in his personal life as well as his business.

He was among the Prestige Group's high-profile clients she'd be meeting this evening in this elegant executive reception room at Houston's newest five-star hotel, the Sterling Uptown.

Since Wynter had been hired more than a month ago, she'd spent hours studying their clients' images and selection criteria in order to earn the respect of her boss, Hope Malone. Hope's matchmaking firm almost exclusively catered to the world's richest and most powerful people: rock stars, A-list actors, politicians, royalty, and business magnates.

SIERRA CARTWRIGHT

Recently a whole new avenue had opened up to Hope through her mentor. The fact she was marrying Rafe was an added bonus.

Rutherford was a Titan, a member of the exclusive Zeta Society.

Like the rest of Prestige's clientele, they were as discerning as they were demanding. But only Rutherford completely captivated her.

Which made no sense at all.

The man—whom Prestige had been courting for months —was the exact opposite of the kind of man Wynter was attracted to.

Shaking her head to clear it of his searing image, she switched to his profile.

Rutherford was from the upper echelons of American society, a direct descendent of the first man to make his fortune from oil. Some online paparazzi sites referred to him as an American prince.

In his criteria for a partner, Rutherford noted he preferred a woman who was interested in having two children, though one was acceptable. As he had the means to hire nannies and tutors, his wife was free to live her own life or pursue her career. Divorce wouldn't be an option unless all children were in college or if there were no children at all within the first five years of their marriage.

Any marriage would be a business arrangement. Nothing more.

His requirements were as cold-hearted as his eyes.

Which meant he was the exact type of man Wynter had no interest in.

Like him, she was from a family of means. But that's where the resemblance ended.

After everything she'd gone through, she would never be

satisfied with a sterile relationship drawn up by lawyers on some piece of paper.

No matter what, she'd hold out for everything. Romance. A home filled with laughter and memories, homework and first dances, puppies and chaos. Happiness.

"Trying to wow the boss?"

"Always." Jolted out of her reverie by her mentor, Skyler, Wynter grinned and closed the app she'd been studying.

Tonight was her first big event—Prestige's Spring Fling. Their most important clients had been invited, along with potential dates for each.

As the firm's newest and most junior matchmaker, Wynter's nerves were on edge. Not only did she want to do an excellent job, she had something to prove.

"Sorry." Wynter slid her phone into her dress pocket. "I didn't see you come over."

"Work or pleasure?"

Wynter scoffed. "What do you think?" Outside of work, neither of them had much of a life.

"Figured." Skyler sighed. "I was hoping you had a beau of your own."

"Where would I have found one? In all of my spare time?"

"Coffee shop? Or yoga class. Maybe while you're out for a run along Buffalo Bayou."

She laughed. Skyler had her pegged. She'd just named the few places Wynter ever went, besides her mom and stepfather's house. And there, chaos reigned. She had one sister, two stepsiblings, and four half-siblings. Honestly there was nowhere she'd rather hang out.

"We need to have a girls' night. Or spa day."

"That I could go for." Wynter had recently spent so much time at her desk, hunched over a computer screen, that pampering sounded good.

"I'll figure it out. Maybe Hope would like to go with us."

"That would be great." She adored her boss and was glad to have been hired on, despite her lack of experience. Not that there were a lot of college courses in matchmaking. Still, Hope had liked the fact Wynter was an attorney and could be persuasive.

"So…" As always, Skyler was persistent. "Who were you looking at?"

"Everyone on the list, honestly."

"Mmm hmm." Skyler was too perceptive to let that pass. "You were pretty intent."

"Lucas Rutherford."

"Ah. He's the biggest—" She clamped her mouth shut.

They had a rule not to speak badly about their clients. People had their personal reasons for wanting specific characteristics in a spouse—all of them valid. Serving that niche made the Prestige Group successful.

Skyler grinned. "I meant to say he's focused."

Calculating was more like it. Over the years, Wynter had heard plenty of rumors about him.

He had two divorces behind him, though the details of the dissolutions were clouded in mystery. Neither of his exes had spoken to the press. No doubt due to an excellent nondisclosure agreement and an iron-clad prenuptial arrangement.

His professional life, however, was a different story.

In an interview with *Scandalicious*, a favorite online gossip magazine, he'd referred to himself as a Takeover Specialist.

At the polite, ridiculous term, she'd rolled her eyes.

Others called him a plundering bastard.

That description fit him much better.

Business magazines said he was a ferocious private equity investor. He acquired companies, ruthlessly stripped them down, restructured debt, streamlined operations—code-word: fired most of the employees—then resold the downsized company at a significant profit. Along the way, he'd made plenty of enemies.

According to what she'd read this afternoon, his father was demanding Lucas bring his company under the corporate umbrella and take his rightful place in the family business. Which meant he needed an heir.

And it was Wynter's job to find the mother of his child.

"Mr. Rutherford spoke to Hope today. He wants to be married this year. If he hasn't gone on any dates by the middle of May, he's pulling his contract with us. Evidently he doesn't want to take his sister as his plus-one to Hope's wedding."

"What?" Since it was already April, Wynter blinked. "That's only a few weeks. Are you serious?"

"Evidently a smaller company is trying to poach him. That's why I was looking for you. Hope wants you to introduce him to his potentials."

*"Me?* No. No, no, *no."* Skyler couldn't be serious. Wynter was not ready for that kind of responsibility.

"Tony and I both have a full roster tonight. Hope promised Mr. Rutherford personal attention. She'll be there, but she has to act as the hostess. You know how much everyone wants a piece of her attention."

That was true. As a Titan in her own right, she was a powerful force.

But until this moment, Wynter's only job was to mingle with all the attendees, smiling, being courteous and helpful, something her upbringing ensured she did well. But taking on Rutherford by herself...? "What if I work with your clients and you can deal with—"

"Look, Wynter, you've been trained by the best." Widening her eyes, Skyler pointed to herself. "Am I right? Or am I right?"

Wynter couldn't help but laugh. "You've got a point."

"You won't feel totally confident for your first few events. None of us did. But we need your help."

Which was why she'd been hired.

After Hope had gotten engaged to hotel magnate Rafe Sterling, her business had boomed. Prestige had expanded to a larger office space. Hope had also promoted Skyler and her associate, Tony, hired several part-time employees, and crowned Miriam as executive administrator, though she deserved the title of Prestige goddess.

After brushing back her long hair that sported pink stripes tonight, Skyler checked her watch. "You've got about ten more minutes to prep. He'll have five potentials here tonight."

Which gave Wynter about one-hundred twenty seconds to learn as much as she could about each woman she needed to introduce him to.

Around them, activity was winding down.

The jazz trio finished warming up on the bandstand. The catering staff was pouring champagne, the finishing touches were being added to the canape table, and the dessert station was laden with the most incredible delights the French pastry chef had concocted, including small hazelnut opera cakes with the Prestige logo airbrushed on top.

"Hope will want to debrief us before the first guest arrives."

"Which means time's wasting."

Skyler waggled her fingers and walked away to join Tony who stood in front of a bank of windows watching as the setting sun glinted off downtown Houston's spectacular skyscrapers.

Now that she was alone and her heart was racing out of control, Wynter drew a deep breath to steady her nerves. *This is just a job.* She'd represented clients in court. This had to be easier than that.

Or at least that's the story she told herself.

Aware of time slipping away, Wynter reopened the app that had been created for Prestige Group employees. Because it was still in beta testing, the portal had occasional glitches. But it allowed her to view her client and his prospects.

Wynter clicked on the picture of the first potential—Dr. Natalie Swenson—and committed her name and occupation, surgeon, to memory. To his credit, Rutherford's must-haves were almost nonexistent. He was okay with a wide age range and had no specific requests as far as body type or personality.

Hope's intuition—assisted by her AI assistant profiler— had come up with numerous candidates, all accomplished and in a narrow age range of late twenties to mid-thirties. Like Rutherford, they were looking for an uncomplicated personal life while reaping the benefits of having a family and children.

Prospect number two was on track to become a partner at an investment brokerage. A third was a bank VP. The fourth was trained as an attorney who had political ambitions.

Finally she swiped through to the last prospect, an heiress with wealth exceeding Rutherford's. In addition to having a child, she intended to keep her jet-setting lifestyle—with or without a husband—and she had her own unbelievably detailed prenuptial requirements.

From her limited experience, Wynter knew her main responsibility was to introduce Rutherford to his potentials. She needed to stay close in case he didn't click with someone or a potential match tried to dominate his time. If he showed any interest in a candidate, the ever-efficient Miriam was happy to make date arrangements. *Easy peasy.*

Wynter scrolled back to Rutherford's profile one more time and began to read it, this time more carefully. He was no longer a billionaire who'd be in attendance and that she would be talking to. He was her first-ever client.

There was an asterisk next to his requirements. Curious, she clicked on the icon to read more. Instead of loading, an hourglass appeared on the screen along with the word *Loading*.

Before she had the chance to reload or push the Back button, Hope entered, striding purposefully across the ballroom wearing a little black dress that was a perfect mix of professional and dressy. As always, she complemented her look with several gorgeous pieces of jewelry, most of them gifts from her future husband.

"I need everyone over here, please." She waved, signaling her group to join her near the dessert table.

"Before we open the doors, I wanted to thank you all for your excellent work. Despite the move and upheaval, we had our best quarter yet. Your next paycheck will reflect a bonus to say thank you. Oh and two days off."

Tony—wearing his fluorescent pink tie embroidered with white daisies—lifted a mock glass in a toast. "Here, here!"

"Does that include me?" asked Miriam, the newly minted office manager.

"Of course it does. Just because I say we can't survive without you doesn't mean you never get a day off."

Miriam laughed. "I figured that you getting us all a room tonight was the bonus for everything."

"That's because I can, and I know it will be a late night."

"And so we can drink all the champagne later," Skyler added.

The ultraposh property was owned by none other than Rafe Sterling, Hope's fiancé. It was spectacular in every way —one more gem in the chain's crown of exclusive holdings. Though Wynter had grown up in luxury, this stunned her.

Skyler snagged a purple macaron and popped it in her

mouth. "Oh God. Lemon lavender. You've got to try one, Hope."

The two constantly led each other into temptation with doughnuts and other sweets. And when they were desperate, they dove into Tony's not-so-secret stash of M&M's. Unfortunately for her slacks, Wynter joined them far more often than she should.

Hope glanced at the tray as if debating. But she restrained herself. Instead she shook her head. "Perhaps later."

"If there are any left." Evidently unwilling to take the risk, Skyler selected a petit fours.

After a last, rueful glance at the table, Hope returned her attention to the small group of employees. "Is everyone clear on their assignments?"

Tony nodded while Skyler took a bite.

Wynter cleared her throat. "I've got Lucas Rutherford."

"That's right. Thank you for handling him. He's a VIP."

"It's uhm…"

"What's up?" Hope frowned. "Is everything okay?"

"It's a big responsibility."

Skyler brushed crumbs off her hands and addressed Hope. "I've told her she's ready."

"Sorry for throwing you in the deep end, but I need the backup." As always Hope was empathetic, but firm in her convictions. It was the type of strong leadership that Wynter admired. "I know it feels sudden, but Skyler is right. You've been with us for a while, and it's not your first meet and greet."

Wynter preferred the more informal mixers, where a lot of people were invited and clients mingled with anyone they chose. On more than one occasion, guests had paired up and left without ever saying hello to any of the guests of honor.

Tonight's gathering was much more formal. Prestige

clients were invited to arrive at the same time, and their potentials were scheduled at twenty-minute intervals.

"Consider yourself lucky. My first solo gig was a television appearance."

At Skyler's words, Wynter shuddered. That was close to her worst nightmare.

"We'll all keep an eye on you," Tony reassured her.

The banquet manager joined them. "Are you ready, Ms. Malone? You have a couple of guests waiting for the doors to open."

"On my way. Thank you." Hope took a last rueful look at the dessert table. "Let's touch base when everything wraps up."

Skyler flashed a cheeky grin. "You'll find me right here packaging the leftovers to take up to my room. Those chocolate covered strawberries are mine, all mine."

"I don't eat sweets." Tony's lie was as quick as it was blatant, though it wasn't obvious from his trim waist. No one knew exactly how many hours a day he worked out.

"Skyler and Tony, I'd like you in the lobby area to greet people. Miriam and Wynter, you're in here with me." Hope signaled to the trio on the stage.

Moments later, soft jazz filled the air.

As prepared as she could be, Wynter pulled back her shoulders.

All of her colleagues greeted their clients. Hope mingled with the prospects who'd arrived. And Wynter stood in the foyer, waiting for Rutherford, who was late if he was going to show at all.

Natalie arrived, and Wynter went to say hello and apologize on Rutherford's behalf.

"Evidently I'm more interested than he is."

"He's been unavoidably detained." The lie flowed more easily than Wynter could have imagined. Since she was already in deep, she plowed ahead. "Mr. Rutherford sends his apologies."

Natalie checked her watch. "My schedule is tight. Please let Mr. Rutherford know I'm no longer interested in meeting him."

"Ah—" Frantically Wynter scanned the room, looking for Hope, who was nowhere around. "I can check on his whereabouts for you?" Surely Miriam or Hope had contact information.

"Not interested."

"Perhaps there's someone else here that I can introduce you to?"

Natalie held up her hand to interrupt any further attempt at discussion. "A friend convinced me this was a good idea. I knew better. If you'll excuse me, I'm due in surgery before the crack of dawn."

"Would you like to stay for a glass of champagne maybe?" She'd try everything possible to buy them a few minutes.

"Thanks. No. I don't drink when I'm this close to having someone's life in my hands."

Wynter admired that. Although they'd just met, she liked the woman and was annoyed as hell at inconsiderate Rutherford. He could have let someone know he was running late and provided an estimated time of arrival. "I promise you, it doesn't usually go like this."

"It's not your fault. But if a man keeps you waiting the first time you've met, it's not a promising start. Is it?"

Though Natalie made an excellent point, Wynter hated for her evening to end this way. "Please accept my apologies." *On behalf of the jerk who's late.* She pulled a business card from her jacket pocket. "If there's anything I can do for you, please reach out to me."

Natalie didn't take it. "It was nice to meet you, Wynter."

Within moments of Natalie's abrupt exit, Hope hurried over. "What happened?"

Not only had the surgeon walked out with a bad impression of Prestige, now Hope was involved in the situation. "Mr. Rutherford isn't here yet, and Dr. Swenson didn't have time to wait. At this point, she has no interest in meeting him."

"These things happen." Though her words were light, she momentarily pressed her lips together. "Don't let it shake you."

It already had.

After Hope moved off to greet a group of new arrivals, Wynter pulled out her phone again to study the next prospect. This time, the app refused to open at all.

Thankfully she remembered the name of the investment broker Rutherford was scheduled to meet.

Before she could make her way to the lobby, an oil tycoon stopped her to ask if Prestige could arrange for him to simultaneously take two women to the Bahamas for two weeks. With a smile, Miriam joined them and took over the conversation.

Wynter was excusing herself when the energy in the room electrified. Tiny hairs on her nape stood at attention. Battling a sense of fight-or-flight, she turned toward the entrance.

*Lucas Rutherford.*

Her heart jumped into hyperspace. In a fraction of a second, she drank him in, in all his devastating glory. The billionaire with his chiseled features and honed muscles stood over six feet tall and wore nothing but black from his blazer to a lightweight turtleneck, slacks, and shoes. His hair was as dark as midnight, and raked back with every strand in place, as if they didn't dare step out of line.

But it was his eyes that riveted her.

Earlier she'd noted the gun-metal gray color. But no photo could capture their searing intensity.

Confoundingly he stole her breath.

As if sensing her scrutiny, he ignored everyone in the room and met her gaze.

Then he tipped his head to one side. Summoning her?

She shouldn't respond. Yet, caught in something she didn't understand, Wynter obeyed his silent command and crossed the room to meet him.

*Think. Think.*

He was a client. And Wynter had an immediate job to do —get him a date before the middle of next month. With his tardiness, he wasn't making it easy for her. Still, she forced herself to be polite. "Mr. Rutherford."

"I haven't had the pleasure." He extended his hand.

The music and conversation became inaudible over the sound of her racing pulse.

There was no graceful way to refuse to touch him. Annoyed at herself for trembling, she accepted. He was strong without overpowering her. Up close, he was even more shockingly handsome than he'd been from across the room.

Realizing he was still waiting for her to introduce herself, she cleared her throat. "Wynter Ferguson. I…" *Stop being ridiculous.* She'd faced down her share of criminals and hostile witnesses. He was no worse. "I work with Hope."

Even after he released her, her hand still tingled.

"Am I to assume you'll be helping her find a mother for my child?" No trace of a smile curved his lips or lit his gray eyes.

He might be the most striking man she'd ever seen, but ice no doubt ran in his veins. "You could always adopt, you know."

"I beg your pardon?"

*Crap.* Why had she said that? Her first job had gone from bad to worse. After this, no doubt Hope would send her home. But since she'd already misspoken, she might as well keep going. "Or hire a surrogate."

"Do you have a volunteer?" He raked his gaze over her, lingeringly, possessively.

Response—warm and feminine—flooded her. The idea of having sex with him... *God.* No. Where had that ludicrous thought come from? Even if it were allowed, she would never sleep with a man as cold and ruthless as he was.

Still refusing to release her from his spell, he repeated himself. "Do you?"

Somewhere, she'd lost track of the conversation. "Do I what?"

"Know a volunteer surrogate?" His lips twitched as he mocked her.

Wynter fought to gather the frayed edges of her composure by artfully dodging his question while changing the subject. "We have four candidates who are interested in meeting you."

"What happened to the fifth?"

She could—should—come up with a half-truth. But she didn't bother. "Your first match left when you didn't show up on time. No interest in rescheduling."

"That's...unfortunate."

He had nothing else to say? "It is. She was lovely."

"Doubly unfortunate then." His neutral tone indicated he was supremely unconcerned. He turned his wrist to check his watch. If her guess was right, it was the new Bonds device she had recently seen advertised. "Which means we have about ten minutes to get to know each other before my next prospect arrives. Is that correct?"

This was a man she had no interest in getting to know. In her peripheral vision, she caught sight of Hope heading their direction. She had never been more grateful for an interruption.

"Lucas! Glad you're here."

"Sorry." He kissed her on the cheek. "Ms. Ferguson informs me I'm late."

At the direct hit, Wynter winced.

But Hope backed her up. "She's right."

"My apologies all around." His eyes like molten mercury, he looked directly at Wynter. "Can you forgive me?"

He was smooth. She had seen exactly this kind of charisma before. On the witness stand and in front of the jury box. It didn't excite her.

Had Hope noticed the same thing that Wynter had—that he'd offered no reason or excuse? Instead he relied on his charm to excuse his behavior. And she had little tolerance for it. "I'm sure you won't let it happen again."

He looked at Hope. "She is tough."

Hope laughed. "It's probably time someone called you out." A woman walked into the ballroom, followed a few seconds later by a man, both looking around, presumably for Hope. "Work calls. I'll leave you in Wynter's capable hands."

"I'm looking forward to it." His voice was gruff, and a shiver of intimacy fluttered through her.

Hope pasted on a warm smile and went to greet the new arrivals, leaving Wynter alone with Rutherford.

Suddenly she wished she'd been fired so she could escape.

"You've made up your mind about me. Fair enough. I'm accustomed to it." His words held a slight accusatory note. "There are many societal advantages to being married."

Which she knew. Before she'd done any work as a matchmaker, she'd studied the science and art of the things it took to be a successful couple. Around the world, couples routinely married someone who their families had selected.

And those marriages tended to last—far beyond some people she knew.

He was also right about the advantages, not just from a tax perspective, but from societal expectations of certain jobs, like a career in politics. Not that it wasn't possible without a spouse, but some people liked to present a perfect, polished image. Having a partner to share the joys and tribulations of life and parenthood was something many of their clients also desired.

"I fully intend to support my wife and child. Or better, children. Financially as well as emotionally."

"Of course." She should probably apologize. But she didn't.

"How long do we have before the next woman unfortunate enough to have to meet me arrives?"

She exhaled. "Mr. Rutherford, I think we may have gotten off on the wrong foot."

"You said exactly what you wanted to."

In doing so, she'd crossed all kinds of boundaries. "Well…"

"Refreshing."

Unsure what to say, she smoothed the front of her dress.

"Why haven't I seen you before?"

She met his inscrutable gaze. Calling on all her inner resolve, she didn't look away. "I'm new."

"And…" He frowned. "Did you come from another service?"

"Not exactly."

As if confident she'd go on, he waited. Silence grew and stretched until it closed around them. Over the years, she'd used the technique to get people to talk. It had never worked on her. Until now. "A mutual friend sent my resume to Hope."

"What captured her interest? Other than you being plainspoken?"

"You'll have to ask her."

He inclined his head as if acknowledging her nonanswer. "What gives you the qualifications to help me out?"

"Nothing." She shrugged. "No one else was available. I drew the short straw."

"More honesty."

"You seem like a man who appreciates it."

"That's the first thing you've been right about this evening."

He leaned in a little closer, nothing much, but enough to slam her senses into hyperawareness.

"Maybe I can change your opinion of me."

Why was her heart beating so fast? "I wouldn't count on it, Mr. Rutherford."

"No? You don't think so?"

Oh God. His quick smile promised he was taking her words as a challenge.

Thankfully his next potential arrived and was immediately greeted by Hope.

Seconds later, the two walked over.

Wynter desperately needed some space from his overwhelming presence. "Allow me to introduce you to Sasha. She's a partner at an investment brokerage."

"No interest."

Wynter blinked. "What?" How could he possibly not want to meet the gorgeous, successful woman?

"We've…met." He inclined his head as he grinned. "I will guarantee she has no desire to spend one minute in my company."

She understood the sentiment.

At that moment, Sasha looked at Rutherford. Even from across the room, her sudden scowl was clear.

"Sasha worked for a company I acquired."

Wynter read between the lines. "You fired her."

With an easy shrug, he responded, "It was nothing personal."

Hope snagged two glasses of champagne from a tray, then accompanied Sasha from the ballroom.

"I think this calls for a drink," Rutherford said.

Since he was her responsibility, she gritted her teeth before offering to fetch him a champagne.

"I prefer whiskey."

Of course he did. Which meant a trip to the bar.

While she was waiting, Hope joined her. "Crisis averted."

"We've struck out with the first two candidates."

The bartender slid a crystal glass toward Wynter.

"Which is why we have five. And why Lucas needs a dedicated matchmaker all to himself."

"Can I get an assistant?"

Hope laughed. "We really threw you to the wolves, didn't we?"

Wynter just hoped she didn't get devoured.

"Are you doing okay?"

"Yes." Surprisingly. Despite her efforts, every feminine instinct responded to Lucas Rutherford. A small part of her was even enjoying their pointed exchanges.

"Let's hope the next three work out better."

She returned to his side and offered him the drink with its generous pour.

Their fingers brushed, shooting electricity through her.

"Thank you. I always enjoy a beautiful woman serving me."

Scandalized, she allowed her mouth to fall open. "You didn't just say that."

"I most assuredly did."

Could their time together be any more surreal? "A bit of a male chauvinist, Mr. Rutherford?"

"It goes two ways. I treat ladies with the utmost respect." After taking a sip, he leaned toward her, crowding her space, but she refused to pull back. "And I serve her in return. Power. The ultimate aphrodisiac."

She should sever the connection of their gazes, but she remained where she was, captivated, ensnared by his charisma.

Rutherford's next prospect arrived early, and Wynter had never been more grateful to see anyone.

Since Hope and Miriam were both busy, she promised to be right back.

The bank VP and Rutherford talked for longer than their allotted time, something Wynter took as a win. No doubt she needed one.

The last two also went well. Hopefully he'd made arrangements with at least one of the women. If luck were on her side, she'd never have to deal with him again.

But of course he had to be difficult.

At the end of the function, he was standing at a bar-height cocktail table, nursing the last sip of his drink.

"How did it go?" Wynter asked.

"They were not what I was hoping for."

"Oh?" She could not have been more shocked. "In what way?"

"The blonde was too tall."

He towered way above Wynter's own five feet six. "So are you." The candidate had been, at the most, five eight.

"Too tall," he reiterated.

As far as she remembered he hadn't expressed a height preference on his questionnaire. She swallowed her sigh before it escaped. "And number four?"

"Which one was that?"

"The attorney."

"I don't like lawyers. Don't have a lot of use for them. Overpriced. Necessary evil." He grinned.

It wasn't possible for him to know she used to practice law, was it?

"And Marlene? The one who just left?"

"Too high maintenance."

She had to give him that one. The heiress had swept in with her perfect hair, teeth, nails, and tan to go with the fluffy white dog in an oversize purse. "I'll get with Hope, and we'll be in touch with you as soon as we can to set up some more meetings. We have a mixer coming up in the next few—"

"I consider my time successful, Ms. Ferguson. I met someone I'd like to take out."

How was that possible? She'd had him in her sights from the moment he arrived.

"You."

*"What?"* Despite her attempts to maintain her professional demeanor, her voice bordered on hysteria. This had to be his idea of a cruel, cruel joke. "No." She shook her head. Her next words rushed out before she could stop them. "Absolutely not."

When he smiled, it was quick and lethal. "In that case, I'm afraid you're stuck with me as a client for now."

# CHAPTER TWO

W ishing she could kick off the sandals that were killing her feet, Wynter settled for accepting her first glass of champagne for the evening.

The Prestige team had regathered near the dessert table. True to her word, Skyler had piled chocolate-covered strawberries at least a mile high on an oversize plate, and she snatched up the very last petit fours.

Hope addressed them. "I'll make this quick. I know everyone is tired, but since we're not working tomorrow, I want to have a quick debrief while things are still fresh."

Wynter was grateful she didn't have to drive home after the grueling evening.

"Overall, I think the evening was a success. Tony, how did you do?"

"Everyone agreed to at least one meeting next week."

"Excellent." Next, Hope glanced toward Skyler, who'd just swallowed her last bite.

"I'd say pretty good."

Was Wynter the only one who had struck out?

With a grin, Skyler continued. "Miriam told me that Mr.

Martinson wants to take two of his potentials to the Bahamas next week."

"You're kidding, right?" Hope blinked. The octogenarian had outlived his first spouse, then divorced three more. "Both of them? At the same time? Or one after the other?"

Everyone looked to Miriam to fill in the details. "Together. Evidently both potentials are agreeable."

"That's…" Hope seemed to search for the right response. "Unusual. I need to think about this one."

"I told him you'd be in touch."

After nodding and promising to call him in the morning, Hope looked at Wynter. "Any luck with Lucas?"

Heat crept up her cheeks. "Uhm…" Did she really want to confess to her boss that he'd asked her out? Since she'd refused, was it important? "None of his potentials met his criteria." Which was accurate, just fluffed a little around the edges. "Sorry."

"I know he's a tough client. You did as well as any of us would have."

Skyler nodded. "Totally agree."

"Don't worry about him. I'll follow up tomorrow and set something else up for him."

"About that…?"

Hope waited for Wynter to go on.

"He said I was stuck with him."

"That's promising. It must mean he trusts you and enjoyed working with you. We'll chat about it more when you're back in the office on Monday." Then she once again addressed her team. "I've kept you long enough. See you next week."

When the gathering broke up, Skyler picked up her plate. "I'm going to head to the lobby to relax. Anyone want to join me?"

Hope shook her head, but Miriam and Tony both said yes.

"How about you, Wynter?"

"Thanks, but I'm going to head upstairs." And no doubt replay—again and again—every single awful thing that had happened with her only client. When she made mistakes, her brain grinded on them.

Skyler and Tony each snagged a couple of half-full bottles of champagne while Wynter settled for filling her flute all the way to the rim and then taking a small sip so she didn't spill on her way to her room.

After saying goodnight, she walked—or more like limped—toward the elevators. Once she was inside, thankfully alone, she gave into the urge to slip out of her shoes. Balancing her glass, she picked them up, slinging the straps over her index finger.

The elevator dinged, and she moved toward the parting doors, only to have the gorgeous, annoying-as-hell Lucas Rutherford fill the space.

Confused, breathless, she glanced at the numbers. She'd almost exited on the wrong floor. But that might have been better than being confined in such a small space with her nemesis.

Before she had the chance to gather her wits and respond to her survival instinct's demand that she run, the doors closed and the compartment shot skyward, trapping her inside with him.

Of course he stood unreasonably close to her.

Electricity hummed between them. And, oh God, his spicy, masculine scent seemed to sear the air as well as her senses.

He pressed his finger to a small scanner pad, and the penthouse button lit up.

"Tough day?"

*Was that empathy in his voice?* Since she wasn't sure that he was capable of it, she immediately dismissed the thought. More like he was mocking her. "One of the roughest."

"You did fine."

She looked at him. For the first time since she'd met him, his eyes were lighter, and his broad shoulders were relaxed. A softer, more approachable Lucas was eminently more dangerous than the coldhearted one.

"I may have not been at my best either."

It took all of her self-control not to gawk at him. "Was that an apology?"

His lips twitched. "No."

*Of course it wasn't.*

"I figured you would have gone home for the evening."

"My friend Rafe owns the property. He invited me to try it out. Since I was here for the meet and greet, I figured I'd avail myself of his renowned hospitality."

Of course he knew Rafe. No doubt that's why he and Hope were friends as well.

The elevator glided to a stop at her floor, and she darted toward the exit. Her upbringing dictated she should say something polite on her way out, wish him a nice evening or something, but she threw manners to the side just like he did.

Once she left the elevator, she forced herself to continue toward her room instead of giving into the temptation of turning around and looking at the handsome scoundrel one last time.

Her room was cool and welcoming. After dropping her shoes inside the closet, she continued outside onto her small, private balcony.

The temperature was still in the 80s, with a southerly breeze. Humidity hung in the air, warm and thick.

Ten stories below her were a gorgeous pool and hot tub, surrounded by lounge chairs, several tables, and a few private cabanas. The decking featured lots of potted plants and even a couple of palm trees. The lighting was subdued and welcoming, turning the water a beautiful, inviting blue.

Swimming was an activity she didn't get to indulge in often enough, but something that really helped her to unwind and relax.

For a long while, she leaned against the rail, sipping her champagne while enjoying the sights and laughter of the group of people playing an impromptu, informal game with a volleyball.

As she'd predicted, her mind spiraled back in time, and images of Lucas Rutherford once again flooded her mind.

Had she ever met a man more irritating than he was?

The truth was, she probably had. She'd spent her early, formative years around the city's elite.

So what was it about Rutherford, in particular, that annoyed her so much?

Probably her sizzling attraction to him.

Years ago she'd made her choices about the kind of person she wanted to be involved with

Her parents had the kind of marriage Rutherford said he wanted—one where everyone understood the rules and love was ground to dust beneath the heel of obligation.

They'd had two kids, as agreed before they got married. But her mom loved everything about being a parent and wanted more children. Her father refused.

Wynter didn't recall hearing any fights about it. In fact, anger annoyed her father—he considered it a waste of energy. The rare times her mother had cried, he'd chillingly told her not to embarrass herself.

Wynter's mother had given up and divorced him after twelve years of marriage. A short time later, she'd started to date a widower with two kids of his own.

They'd moved in together and had four more kids.

Pandemonium had echoed through the smallish house, and so had laughter. When she spent time at her mom and stepfather's, she was happy.

When she graduated from high school, her father had expressed disappointment in her choice of colleges as he'd gifted her with a stock portfolio. But her mother and extended family had thrown her a party complete with ridiculous gag gifts, games, flowers, a sash, a tiara, and a homemade cake.

It was in that moment that Wynter decided she would lead with her heart and not her head when it came to the man she'd marry.

Which made her primal attraction to Lucas Rutherford even more annoying.

In frustration, she finished her drink, then wandered back inside to lose herself in a mindless show on television. An hour later, she was still flipping through the channels, and nothing had held her attention.

Restless, she strode back to the balcony. The raucous group had left the pool area. The clouds from earlier had parted, and moonlight glinted off the water, beckoning her.

Knowing she needed to burn off her abundance of energy if she had any hope of sleeping, she changed into her swimsuit, then wrapped herself in a white, waffle weave robe embroidered with the Sterling Uptown logo before heading for the elevator.

There were a couple of people in the far away hot tub, but the pool itself was empty, allowing her the freedom to swim laps.

Since her only focus was on shutting down her thoughts, she logged the first ten at top speed, setting an exhausting pace.

Then she slowed down, making each stroke a meditation, focusing on her breathing and form.

She pushed through the first waves of fatigue, continuing for as long as she had energy and until there was nothing but her, the night air, and the refreshing water.

Much more at ease, she allowed herself a cooldown period before making her way toward the side. A soak in steamy water would be a nice way to end the night and relax completely.

Before she could hoist herself up, a powerful hand clamped around her wrist.

She looked up, and her heart rate soared.

*Lucas Rutherford.*

God help her. Mostly naked, chest glistening with droplets of water, wearing only a pair of trunks and a white towel draped around his shoulders, he was even more gorgeous than he had been in a suit. This close, she had no option but to notice his honed biceps and abs. There wasn't an ounce of fat on him anywhere.

"Seems we have something in common after all, Ms. Ferguson." With an effortless pull, he helped her from the water. "A love of the water."

Wynter stood on the decking in front of him, suddenly aware of how skimpy her two-piece suit was and how tiny she was compared to him. He was so broad, and she would easily fit beneath his chin.

Unable to find her voice, she moved to a chair to slip into her robe. She needed the protection.

"Couldn't sleep?"

"I figured a swim and a soak in the hot tub would help me unwind."

"I did both."

She'd been so focused on achieving her goal that she hadn't looked to see if he was anywhere close.

"Nightcap?" He nodded toward a small table with a bottle of very expensive bubbly sitting on it.

"Glass is prohibited in the pool area."

"So it is."

"Are you always a rule breaker, Mr. Rutherford?"

He placed his finger beneath her chin and tipped it back. "Before the night is over, I intend to break a few more."

The combination of his gentle yet firm touch and the hypnotic power of his eyes was deadly. *Why am I still standing here?* She had no desire to fall under his spell, no matter how tempting he was.

"Do you?"

"Starting now." He leaned toward her.

She refused to let him kiss her. "You don't like lawyers, remember?"

"In general, not in specific. I adore a woman who can hold her own."

But when he captured her shoulders and drew her toward him, she responded, rising onto her tiptoes.

"You're beautiful, Ms. Ferguson."

From his lips, in that tone, she believed him.

The first brush of his lips across hers was gentler than she anticipated, the barest of whispers, and it made him irre-sistible.

With exquisite tenderness, restraining his power, he sought entrance to her mouth. He tasted of the smokiness of his earlier whiskey and something headier, of promise and mystery.

Because she rarely dated, she hadn't been kissed often, and never like this.

As their tongues entwined and danced, her senses exploded with excitement. When he placed a palm on the small of her back and brought her against his masculine body —and arousal—every nerve ending came alive.

In his indomitable, ruthless way, he threatened to consume her.

Slowly, with seeming reluctance, he drew away. "If I don't stop now, I'll have to take you up to my room."

Her response to him—raw hunger and desire—left her shaken, and she shook her head. "I…uhm…"

"Ready for that glass of champagne?"

*Run.* But her body refused to obey her mind's instinct. It was as if shared intimacy had woven a spell around her. She didn't want to end the enchantment.

"What can it hurt? Get to know each other a little better. Maybe it'll make it easier for you to find me a wife."

Because she was so discombobulated, she seized on that excuse.

He held her chair while she took a seat. The few other patrons who'd been down here headed toward the exit, leaving them alone in the warm night air, shadowed by the gentle lighting.

After sitting across from her, he poured the champagne into the glasses.

"Were you expecting company?"

"No. The glasses were stacked on top of each other, and I picked up both without thinking. It was a happy coincidence."

She took a small sip. Wynter wasn't sure if it was from her recent exercise or because of his presence, but the bubbles went straight to her head.

Lucas Rutherford was more than just handsome. For the first time, she noticed the wariness that lay buried in the depths of his eyes. Perhaps that was a trick of the light or her imagination. But it intrigued her. "Earlier you suggested I'd made up my mind about you."

"Was I right?"

*Maybe.* His intense scrutiny made her shift. To cover her sudden nervousness, she cupped the glass between her hands. "You've been married before."

"Twice. And you?"

"Nice try. This is about you."

He grinned, making him much more accessible and intriguing than she'd found him before. "In the interest of fairness, I reserve the right to ask you one question before the night is through. Fair?"

She exhaled. And she would have never agreed if she wasn't curious about what he wanted to know. "One and no more."

He nodded. "Ask away."

"What makes you think that third time would be a success?"

"Because my expectations are different."

"In what way?" Curious, she waited for him to continue.

"Soon after I finished grad school, I proposed to the woman I'd been dating for two years." He moved his glass to the side. "We attended school together. But she had no real understanding of my financial circumstances."

"In what way?"

"I refused to join the family business. Because of that, my father was unwilling to help fund my startup company. Priscilla believed we'd have a certain lifestyle. It didn't include an apartment and a shared, secondhand vehicle. It was one thing to live that way while we'd been in school, but not afterward." He shrugged. "I got my business off the ground on a shoestring by raising funds from investors and friends."

"Leverage."

"Risky business, that." He tipped his head to the side to show he agreed with what she said. "My first deal crashed and burned. It would have left us bankrupt if Priscilla hadn't been supporting us. But it was never her intention to be the family breadwinner. And I don't blame her. She had every right to demand that I would provide for her. After a few months of paying the bills, she'd had enough. I put a second deal together, and it was much more successful, but I was working sixteen hours a day, seven days a week. We never saw each other. I paid back every cent I owed her, and I didn't contest the divorce when she asked for it."

Doubts niggled at Wynter. Maybe she shouldn't have asked. The more she knew about him, the more real he became, chipping away at the walls she'd already erected between them.

"And number two." For a moment he stared off into the distance. "Ileana." Then he looked at her, and she read hurt and betrayal in his eyes. "I loved her. The sentiment wasn't returned, though she did everything in her power to cover that up."

At the pain in his tone, Wynter recoiled.

"After the first lie came undone, a dozen more followed."

"I'm…" She wasn't usually at a loss for words, but right now she didn't know what to say. "It had to be difficult."

"Perhaps I could have gotten past some of them. But there was one I will *never* forgive."

The air temperature seemed to have dropped fifty degrees. "It's made you cautious."

An unfriendly smile toyed with his lips. "Jaded? A bastard? Uncaring? An asshole?"

Since all of those thoughts had gone through her mind, she winced.

"Make no mistake." He leaned toward her. "The things you've read about me? Every single thing is true. After I banished Ileana from my life, without a dime of my money, I threw myself into my work. And I used it as the playground to exorcise my demons."

*All of them?* Or did the ghosts of some still haunt him?

"I want a child. That hasn't changed. I'm also enough of a traditionalist to want a family and not a surrogate."

Another direct hit. Not a surprise, really. He'd warned her that everything she'd heard about him was true. "I apologize for that comment."

"No need. As I said, I find your direct manner refreshing. At least you're willing to tell me the truth as you see it."

A few minutes later, she finished her drink, and he offered to walk her back to her room. "Unless you still want to get in the hot tub?"

"Probably not a good idea after drinking." And he might join her.

"Agree." He picked up their glasses and the bottle.

"There's no need for you to leave just because I am."

"On the contrary, Ms. Ferguson. There are certain things a gentleman should always do for the lady he's spending time with."

"It's different when the relationship is a business arrangement." She stood. "Lucky for you, you're off the hook."

"Ah. So you'd like to pretend that kiss never happened, would you?"

Heat chased through her, and she knew it had nothing to do with the bubbly she'd just enjoyed. "I think that would be for the best."

"When I kicked Ileana out of my life, I vowed I would never tolerate deception ever again. So you can admit it affected you." He shrugged. "Or you can lie, knowing that I see straight through it."

"Mr.—"

"Lucas."

Feeling a little trapped, caught in the half-truth, she boldly met his gaze. "You asked for it. It was amazing. And that's exactly why you should not walk me back to my room. I prefer to put some distance between us."

"I respect that." He stood. "You may think I am a barbarian, and there are times you'd be correct, but I have some familiarity with the concept of manners."

How had he seen through everything that she'd said since the moment they'd met?

"I'll walk you to your room."

Since arguing would get her nowhere, she relented.

Being in the elevator with him was no easier the second time around. In fact being in such a small space now that she'd tasted his possession was worse than before.

When they reached her room, he placed the glasses and champagne on the floor, then backed her against the door and placed his hands on either side of her head. "You owe me the answer to my question."

She'd forgotten her rash promise.

"I only want to know one thing. How has no man scooped you off the market?"

Thought was impossible when he stood so close, invading her space, igniting her senses?

"Hmm?"

Knowing he'd see through any subterfuge, she revealed as much as she was willing to, while keeping her privacy. "Like you, I don't date a lot. But I haven't found a man who will give me exactly what I want."

"And what is that?"

Fighting to keep control of the situation, she shook her head. "I promised you one question. And I answered it."

Obviously realizing he'd been bested, he grinned. "So you did."

She turned, and he stepped back. Thank God. She wasn't sure what she would have done if he had leaned in to kiss her a second time. Would she have possessed the resolve to push him away?

Wynter pressed her finger to the touchpad to release the lock.

He didn't leave, even when she closed the door behind her.

For long moments she remained in the foyer, frozen in place, unable to believe that the past hour had actually happened.

She brushed her fingertip across her lips. They still felt swollen, but that might be her overactive imagination.

Her mind still reeling, Wynter showered. Once she'd dried off, she pulled on her sleep T-shirt. She'd gone downstairs hoping that she'd be able to unwind enough to sleep, but she was more keyed up than she'd ever been. No man had affected her this powerfully.

Her earlier fear had been realized. Getting to know him had been a monumental mistake.

So why did she still want to learn more?

She pulled back the covers and sat cross-legged on the bed before giving in to temptation and opening her work app.

Even as she told herself she shouldn't be doing this, she scrolled to Lucas's profile and read his information with fresh eyes. Lucas's two divorces now had some context. She might not like the way he did business, but she understood it a little better.

Still, nothing she'd learned would help her do her job any better.

Though he'd told her about himself, there was plenty of missing information.

She continued scrolling lower. This time, when she touched the asterisk, the special requirements section opened.

In shock, her eyes widened. Not only was Lucas Rutherford a ruthless billionaire, he was a Dominant with special requirements.

Wynter's breath threatened to strangle her.

Her best friend, Anna Bella, lived the lifestyle. One weekend when the city had been drenched by a tropical storm, they had binge watched a couple of BDSM-themed movies on a streaming service. Because Wynter had been fascinated, she'd peppered Anna Bella with hours' worth of questions.

They'd talked a lot about what was accurate and what was Hollywood-hype.

Anna Bella had invited Wynter to a couple of events at a Houston club, but she'd never gotten up the courage to attend.

While she knew Prestige catered to clients who were interested in D/s, it hadn't occurred to her that Lucas was into it.

Suddenly her mind spiraled backward, and she recalled the way she instinctively responded to him and his unspoken command when he first arrived in the ballroom. And his pleasure when she fetched his whiskey.

All the signs were there, and she'd missed them.

Scandalized, she dropped the phone beside her.

Of course she hadn't known. Wynter had no submissive tendencies and zero real-life exposure to his way of life.

She was certain, though, that she had little interest in catering to his needs. Or were they demands?

"No, no, *no.*" She couldn't allow her thoughts to gallop down that path.

More than ever, she realized she had to stay away from him. If she succumbed to his commanding aura, he would surely destroy her.

Picking up her phone once more, she sent Hope a text message. *I can't work with Mr. Rutherford. I'm sorry.*

Then she jumped out of the bed to pace the room, anxious for her boss's response.

When her phone dinged, Wynter snatched it up.

*I enjoyed sharing a drink and conversation.*

Lucas. But how had he gotten her phone number?

At the absurd thought, she shook her head. He was a Titan, and that meant he had contacts everywhere.

*I made us reservations for breakfast. Pool deck at eight o'clock?*

# CHAPTER THREE

"You met someone you wanted to take on a date?"

"I did." Last night, after inviting Wynter to breakfast, Lucas had sent a message to Hope requesting a brief meeting at seven a.m.

She'd responded that she'd be there, along with her fiancée.

Now, across the table at La Patisserie, the hotel's specialty coffee and confectionary shop, Lucas studied her. Since many people were sleeping or having room service, the place was relatively quiet.

"Congratulations. Then I'll consider the meet and greet a success."

"Hold the accolades until you hear the rest. It's...complicated."

"Why am I not surprised?" She broke off a chunk of chocolate-drizzled biscotti and dunked it into her coffee.

"I plan to pursue Wynter."

"What?" Hope dropped the cookie. After bouncing around for a few seconds, it floated to the top.

Interesting. Until now, he believed she was unflappable. "Is it against the rules?"

"Would it stop you if it were?"

"No." Lucas grinned. "I would happily pay the termination fee to get out of your ridiculously expensive contract."

Using her spoon, she fished out the soggy piece of pastry. "Tell me again how expensive a divorce is? Or a disastrous marriage?"

"Oof." Rafe grinned. "She has you there."

"Touché." Lucas grimaced. She knew what her services were worth, and she didn't discount her fees. The business executive in him admired her shrewdness.

"Does Wynter know?"

Oh yes. He'd made his attraction to the stunning blonde abundantly clear. And their shared kiss had solidified his desire.

In the aftermath, her enticing blue eyes—the color of a sun-kissed summer day—had been wide open with a tremor of fear dancing there. She wanted him even though instinct whispered that he was dangerous as fuck. And he was. This morning, when he showered, he remembered how swollen her pretty pink lips had been, and he wanted to see them bruised from being crushed beneath his.

One thing was certain, he intended for her to be the mother of the beautiful children they would make.

"Lucas?"

Jolted, realizing Hope was waiting for an answer, he grinned. "I'm not known for my subtlety."

"You don't say." Hope's words were flat. "How did she respond?"

*With a hell no.* "Not as favorably as I would like."

"I see."

He frowned. "What are you not saying?"

Before responding, Hope and Rafe had a quick silent

exchange, then she leveled a cold, hard stare at Lucas. "What happened after the event was over?"

"We ran into each other and shared some champagne at the pool."

"Glass is prohibited there," Rafe pointed out.

"So I've been told."

Scowling at them both, Hope sighed. "Go on."

He omitted the fact he'd kissed her and that she'd responded, and that he'd been unable to forget the sweet taste of her, or the way she'd so perfectly yielded to his touch. It had been years since he'd lost sleep over a woman, even longer since he'd masturbated three times in twelve hours.

"Anything else?"

He didn't care about his reputation—events and scandal rags had already tarnished it enough. But he'd die to protect Wynter's. "I was a perfect gentleman."

"Were you?" She picked up her cup and regarded him over the rim. "Then why did she contact me, refusing to keep you as a client?"

"Did she?" The news delighted him. If he hadn't unnerved her, she would have no reason to fire him. "And I will not work with any other matchmaker at Prestige."

"Lucas—"

"Nonnegotiable, Hope. It's Wynter or no one."

"And my nonnegotiable: I will not force her to have anything to do with you."

"In that case, consider my contract canceled."

She met his gaze, and hers was just as hard as his. "I'll get a confirmation out to you as soon as I'm in the office on Monday. As I stated earlier, you'll be paying the termination fee."

"Understood."

"Look…" She trailed off before starting again. "Friend to friend? This is a bad idea."

Wouldn't be his first.

"I would never pair you two together."

"The five women you found for me weren't a success either."

She sighed. "That's different."

"How so?"

"I used the AI assisted matching process. We weigh *all* of your requirements."

Including a woman who was open to BDSM or understood that he would continue to scene at his favorite clubs.

"We also take into consideration the Three C's—compatibility, chemistry, and commitment."

At their intake appointment, she'd explained exactly how the program worked.

"I'm not going to ask about chemistry between you."

"Good. I wouldn't have answered anyway."

"She's the type of woman who would demand commitment."

"No problem there. I want to get married." As far as he was concerned, they had already checked two of the three required boxes. Those were odds he'd accept all day long.

"Which leaves compatibility. You're not a match there."

"Are you calling me an asshole?"

Instead of answering, Hope smiled.

"You don't pull any punches."

"I will not tell you anything about Wynter that's private. That wouldn't be fair to her. But she's not as callused as you are. And I don't want her to change who she is to accommodate you."

Everything about Wynter attracted him—including her personality. "Nor do I."

"In answer to your earlier question, we have no specific policy preventing associates from dating clients. Though maybe we should."

If he recalled correctly, Rafe had been a Prestige client himself. Now *Scandalicious* gossip magazine had christened them as Houston's newest power couple. Their respect for each other, and their love, was clear.

At one time Lucas had believed that he and Priscilla might share something similar. With their combined talents, they'd have made a formidable team. And now...? He'd settle for a woman who was mostly honest or even disinterested enough in their relationship not to have any qualms about telling him the truth.

"If something works out long-term, I expect you to pay the full fee."

"Even though I'm terminating the contract?"

"You met through Prestige." She shrugged. "Next time read the disclaimers."

His respect level for her nudged up a couple of notches. "You're a shrewd businessperson."

"I will tell you this, Lucas." She moved her beverage aside, then lanced him with a serious stare. "If you hurt her, I will personally kick your ass."

Rafe smiled broadly. "Good luck, buddy. You're going to need it."

The conversation moved away from Prestige and Lucas's personal life and turned toward Rafe and Hope's upcoming nuptials. If his name was still on the guestlist when the May date arrived.

Aware of the passing time, he pushed back his chair. "If you'll excuse me? I have breakfast reservations."

"Here?" Rafe asked.

Lucas nodded. "The pool deck." And because he was a Sterling Premier member, he'd gotten the table he requested.

"I'll send over a bottle of champagne."

"So it *is* permitted if you're serving it."

"It's a safety issue."

Lucas grinned. With that, he stood and said his goodbyes.

Happier, lighter than he'd been in months, he threaded his way to the host stand.

Within three minutes of being seated, a cup of coffee sat in front of him, along with the promised bubbly chilled in a silver ice bucket.

As always, Rafe was impressive.

Half an hour later, he checked his watch and glanced toward Wynter's balcony.

Her door was closed as were the drapes.

Perhaps she was on her way down?

After allowing enough time for her to arrive, he checked his phone. There were no messages and no missed calls.

Until this moment it hadn't occurred to him that she would stand him up.

*Well played, Wynter.*

Undeterred, he told the server he needed to leave, he signed the check, then dropped a significant tip on to the table.

He rode the elevator to her floor and strode to her room.

The door stood open, and the housekeeper stripped the sheets off the bed.

Without him being aware of it, Wynter had fled the hotel.

Quizzically the housekeeper looked at him. "Can I help you, sir?"

"Thank you, no." He shook his head.

More than ever, the feisty Ms. Ferguson had piqued his interest.

And the next move was his.

He hoped she was prepared for his all-out assault.

At a brisk run, Wynter completed her third circuit around Buffalo Bayou. Because it was mid-Saturday and the sun was high, she'd worn a light shirt, shorts, and an Astros ball cap.

Ever since the pre-function meeting where she'd learned that Lucas Rutherford was her client, her nerves had been on edge.

Hope's reassurances that Wynter didn't have to work with him ever again should have soothed her, but it hadn't. Nothing she'd tried all day had vanquished her restlessness.

If she'd slept four hours all night, she'd count it as a miracle.

The man himself consumed her.

Which was why she'd texted her bestie around ten o'clock this morning and asked if they could go for a walk.

Almost every weekend, the two of them got together. Usually she and Anna Bella grabbed a coffee, did a little shopping, or tried a new place to eat. Cocktails were often involved.

Since Anna Bella detested exercise, the heat, and the humidity, she'd added a couple of stipulations. After one lap, they had to find an air-conditioned restaurant. Which was why Wynter had shown up early to log a few miles.

A few minutes before their agreed time, she reached their meeting place below a live oak tree.

Of course Anna Bella hadn't arrived, so Wynter continued jogging.

When she returned, Anna Bella was parked across the street, windows up, evidently enjoying her last few moments of air-conditioned bliss.

Wynter waved her over. Anna Bella wrinkled her nose but climbed out of the vehicle and pulled on a big floppy hat. Then she slathered on a thick layer of sunscreen before grabbing a large bottle of water.

With a quick grin, Wynter hugged her friend.

"Eww. God. Gross. You're sweaty."

"Happens when you exercise."

Anna Bella majored in theater and still participated in community and regional plays. Recently she'd added improv to her arsenal of entertainment. Now, in her typical, exaggerated way, she shuddered.

"At any rate, I prefer the word *glow*."

"Well you're glowing extra hard."

"You ready?"

"Hell no. But yes. Let's get this torture over with as fast as possible."

Which did not mean Anna Bella wanted to run or even jog.

They hit the path, but neither said much until they were away from other pedestrians and a long trail of road bikes.

"I want you to know what you've done to me is not fair."

Slowing her pace, Wynter glanced over at her friend. "Which part?"

"The whole thing. All of it. You texted me at the ass-crack of dawn—"

"It was after ten."

"Whatevs." Anna Bella waved a hand. "You said you had a sucky night and wanted to do a talkie-walkie. First of all, you woke me up."

*"Really?"*

"Okay. No. So I made that up."

"You don't turn your phone on before noon on weekends."

Anna Bella shrugged. "But you didn't tell me what was wrong, and I asked at least ten times."

*True.*

"I don't do cliffhangers. You know I hate them." In movies or books or life.

"But it was effective, right? I mean you're here, and you're walking."

"Which is also not fair."

"I'll buy the coffee."

"I want to go somewhere that we can get it spiked. Baileys or amaretto. Hell, I'm not picky. I'll settle for a chocolate liqueur in a mocha."

Wynter shook her head. No matter what was wrong, spending time with her friend made it better.

"So now that you've got me out of bed, tell me what's going on. Didn't you have a meet and greet last night? And a free room at the Sterling Uptown?"

Which she'd invited Anna Bella to share. But since she'd already had plans to meet others at the local BDSM club, she'd refused. "Yes."

"So what went wrong?"

Wynter spent the next few minutes outlining the fact she'd been assigned to take care of Lucas Rutherford.

*"The* Lucas Rutherford? His Highness, Lucas Rutherford?"

At Anna Bella's comical expression, Wynter laughed. "Yes."

"And? Tell me he's a big fat jerk like I think he is."

"We're not allowed to say anything bad about our clients."

"Ha! I guessed it. He's a royal jerk. Get it? He is called the American prince after all."

At her friend's attempt at humor, Wynter groaned. "That's terrible."

"Nah. Wasn't that bad." They neared a park bench, and Anna Bella plopped herself down on it.

"We've been walking for less than ten minutes."

"It's hot." Anna Bella uncapped her water and drizzled a small amount down her shirt to cool off. "And the conversation is getting interesting."

Not ready for a rest, Wynter remained standing and

began a series of slow stretches. "He didn't approve of any of his matches."

"I'm surprised he wants to get married again if everything I've heard is true."

Wynter didn't respond to that. Since she'd closed her hotel room door between them, she'd read at least a hundred articles about him…even though she'd repeatedly told herself to stop.

"So then what happened? That's not enough to send you into a tailspin."

"We…ah…"

"What?" Anna Bella raised her eyebrows several times in quick succession, making Wynter grin. "Do tell."

"We had champagne poolside."

"Seriously? You had drinks with the billionaire?"

When Wynter nodded, Anna Bella went on. "Just the two of you? Or was it with a group of people?"

"We were alone."

"You've got my undivided attention."

She never intended to mention the kiss, but her confession spilled out in a rush.

"Wait. What?" Anna Bella removed her hat and fanned herself with it. "He freaking kissed you? And was it everything?"

*And more.*

"So he wasn't terrible? Sloppy like a Saint Bernard or anything?"

This was why she needed a constant Anna Bella fix. "Will you stop?"

"And not like a closed-mouthed peck?"

Wynter shook her head.

"Good. Good. Not a pecker. So you liked the kiss. What happened after that?"

"He asked me out."

"He... *What?*"

"Invited me to join him for breakfast."

"Well, his taste in women has improved a lot. I can say that much."

She appreciated her friend's loyalty.

"What did you say?"

"Nothing."

"I'm confused." Anna Bella shook her head. "Did you go?"

"No." A few minutes before eight, she had given into the temptation to peek out the window, just in time to see him get seated at the same table they'd shared last night.

Soon afterward, champagne had arrived.

That's when she made her decision.

The setting, the gentle breeze, bright sunshine, and *him*... Lucas was the picture of understated elegance and power in a blazer and khakis, the top button of his polo shirt unfastened.

In order to save herself, she had to stay far, far away from him.

Hurriedly she finished packing her overnight bag and headed for the valet stand, checking out of her room on the app after she had left the hotel.

"So...?" Anna Bella plopped her hat back into place. "Help me out here. A billionaire treated you to champagne, ravaged you with his kiss, and then asked you to go out on a date. Yeah. Sounds like a sucky evening to me."

In frustration, Wynter looked skyward.

"Oh shit. You're attracted to him, aren't you? And want to call him?"

"*No.*" Her reply was too quick.

"Methinks the lady doth protest too much."

*Maybe.*

"Now I need all the details. You have to fill in the blanks."

"You'll have to walk to get them."

"You are the absolute worst. A mean, evil friend."

"Write me into your next play."

"Don't think I won't. And I'll have your character *glowing* all the time."

At a slower pace than before, they continued down the path. "So the reason I didn't want to talk at a restaurant... I'm curious how you figured out you were into BDSM."

*"What?* His Highness is a Dominant?"

"I'm not talking about him." Because she'd learned that information through work, she couldn't share it with anyone.

"Oh. Sure. It's a coincidence that a man asked you out last night and you have a sudden interest in my personal life."

"Trying to expand my horizons."

"Mmm-hmm. Okay. Fine. I'll play along." A little more spring in her step, Anna Bella grinned. "A guy I went to school with belonged to a club. One evening a bunch of us tagged along with him. I felt as if I belonged. Everything I saw, from the St. Andrew's crosses to the cupping table was a visual feast. And then the sounds... People interacting, but interlaced with the snap of leather and the whimpers and cries of pleasure. The first couple of times I went, I walked around in a little bit of a daze. Sensory overload is the best way to describe it. What really excited me was the fact it's a place with no judgment. We have rules and safe words. But within those confines, everyone gets to express their true nature."

Not sure she understood, Wynter remained silent.

"What?" From beneath the brim of her ridiculous hat, Anna Bella peeked at Wynter. "You have a question; I know you do."

"I guess... I'm confused about what submission is."

"In what way?"

"You kick ass in the real world." Running a theater,

writing plays, raising funds, directing stagehands. She was a formidable force in the Houston arts community.

"Thank you." Anna Bella wrinkled her nose. "At least I think that was a compliment."

Wynter sighed. "I'm trying to be tactful."

"You're crashing and burning." Her smile was quick and wide and teasing. "But, here, let me get you a shovel so you can dig yourself in even deeper."

"I don't picture you as someone who is submissive."

"There are as many ways to have a BDSM relationship as there are people on the planet. I have no interest in being subservient to anyone outside of a club. And a lot of other people share my point of view. Sure there are people who are really into it, like slaves, but that's not the majority of us."

She didn't have to wait long for Anna Bella to go on.

"Submissive has nothing to do with your professional life. We have CEOs, a county sheriff, a CIA agent, and a few judges who bottom at the club."

"Are you serious?"

Anna Bella gave a sassy grin. "I'm sure you've argued in front of some of them."

Oh God, no. "I can't deal with the images that are flashing in my mind."

"There's a few I would like to forget myself."

"That's just... Please tell me one of them isn't Judge Hancock." Wynter never wanted to see what was beneath his black robe.

"My lips are sealed. And so would yours be if you attended the club. Privacy is absolutely guaranteed. And some people opt to use a scene name—meaning just when they're at the club or attending a play party, that sort of thing. In fact, unless we're sure it's okay, we aren't allowed to mention that we know people in real life."

"I had no idea."

"Bottoming—or topping—can be a great stress release. And it wouldn't be if you had to worry about having your kinks broadcast to the world."

"Makes sense."

"So back to your question. I'm not submissive, but at the club…? Oh la la." She raised her shoulders and affected a shiver. "I get to unleash my wildest imaginations and let my freak flag fly."

"So it's all acting?" After all, Anna Bella was accomplished on the stage.

"Not at all. That's not what I'm trying to say." Anna Bella shook her head. "I love roleplay, but I feel as if I'm putting on a show if I'm having vanilla sex. Does that make sense? I want something more, and with most guys, I don't get what I'm craving."

After learning Lucas wanted a relationship with BDSM elements—or a wife who didn't care that he would pursue it outside their marriage—Wynter hadn't been able to sleep.

Watching the movies with Anna Bella had been Wynter's first-ever exposure to BDSM, and they'd baked a couple of frozen pizzas so they could binge the entire trilogy. So obviously she was interested enough to invest over six hours of her time.

Until now, the films and her discussions with Anna Bella had been interesting, but nothing more.

But last night and for most of the day, she hadn't been able to stop picturing Lucas picking up a flogger as he looked at her with his steely eyes.

The images shocked her. Worse—terrifyingly—they aroused her.

"Not everyone finds it the way I do. Some of my friends say they always knew they were a Dominant or a submissive. Or a Top or bottom. And they sought out others like themselves as soon as they could."

Wynter had a vague recollection of discussing this before. "Now I'm confused." Again. "Is a Top a Dominant?"

Anna Bella laughed.

"Not necessarily. A Top may enjoy wielding a whip, for example. Impact play. But he or she may not be Dominant. And not everyone who likes the feel of that single tail on their skin is a submissive. D/s is more of a relationship dynamic between a twosome or moresome. Protocols, behavior expectations, may be in place. Service may be part of it, and it might not. They can live the lifestyle 24/7 or practice at certain times, like when they're alone or on the weekends. There's something for everyone. Like a buffet, you know?"

That idea, Wynter liked.

"But yeah, every time there's a new BDSM movie or best-selling book, more people become aware of the lifestyle. So I'd say a lot of us didn't know it intuitively, but it sparks something inside us, you know?"

Until now, she hadn't.

"There are a vast range of kinks. Some people like bondage and nothing else. At the club there are always demonstrations—and there's an entire art form to it, including suspension. Seeing someone wearing nothing but ropes is breathtaking. And speaking of that..." Anna Bella stopped, took off her hat, and fanned herself with it. "I'm out of breath myself right now. I'm turning back. If you want to melt like the Wicked Witch of the West, go ahead. But I'm getting out of this freaking furnace that is southeast Texas."

And summer was still a couple of months away. "Fine. You win." Between the walk and the drive to their favorite place, they'd have a few more uninterrupted minutes to finish the conversation.

Below them, on the water, kayakers paddled by.

Wynter mentioned she was considering buying one and trying it out.

"Make it a gondola with a man singing to me as he ferries me around, and I'm in. No. Wait. If he also has wine and cheese, I'll do it."

After they stopped to pet a runaway dog and hold it while its owner caught up, they meandered back to their vehicles.

"Where were we? Oh sadomasochism."

She shuddered. "I don't think I'd like that."

"Good to know. A lot of people enjoy impact play for pleasure only."

Was that why she'd imagined Lucas striding toward her, his features set in a purposeful line?

"It's complex, multidimensional. Even after all these years, I'm still not sure I understand everything involved, which is half the fun. Why don't you see for yourself? Come to the club with me tonight?"

No way was Wynter ready for that. "Some other time."

Hours later, when she was back home alone, part of her wished she'd had the courage to accept her friend's invitation. It would be better than trying to keep thoughts of Lucas out of her head.

Around nine o'clock, her phone chimed.

*Missed you at breakfast.*

She should block his number. After all, he was no longer a client.

But then she'd never know if he'd tried to contact her.

*I brought the champagne home with me in case you ever want to share it.*

A million times no.

Her heart raced in irregular bursts. He'd told her he wanted to take her out. Maybe because she'd refused, he was more captivated.

Or perhaps he was attracted to her.

She shook her head as she paced her living room. Impossible. A man such as him could have his choice of any woman on the planet. So yes. He had to want the one he couldn't have.

Wynter didn't sleep any better that night, or Sunday night.

Monday, she arrived at the office bleary eyed and without her customary energy. But since it had been her turn to pick up treats for Prestige's weekly meeting, she headed for the conference room to open the boxes filled with bagels and cream cheese. Unable to help herself, she'd also purchased an enormous selection of kolaches and a few donuts.

"Carb loading in the morning." Tony scanned the offerings. "Tough weekend?"

He had no idea.

From the credenza, she grabbed knives and paper plates. Then she almost bowed down before Skyler when she walked in carrying trays laden with large disposable coffee cups.

"You look like you need this." Skyler found the one with Wynter's name on it and passed it over.

"Thank you." She dropped into a chair and took a long, fortifying sip of the sugary treat.

Within ten minutes, the associates and Miriam were seated around the table. Another meeting would be held this afternoon with the part-timers later to set their weekly assignments.

"Who has updates to share?" After her question, Hope went straight for a donut slathered in chocolate icing.

Miriam spoke up first. "I followed up with Mr. Martinson. He will be taking two of his potentials to the Bahamas this week."

"Good for him." Skyler grinned.

"Hope cleared it with both ladies before I made the flight and hotel arrangements."

Everyone else outlined their action lists, and when it was Wynter's turn, she blushed. "Happy to help anyone who needs it. Or I can work with Miriam on setting up the next mixer."

Skyler leaned forward. "What happened with Mr. Rutherford?"

Rather than waiting for to answer, Hope responded. "He is no longer represented by Prestige."

Wynter gasped. *"What?"* Surely she couldn't have heard correctly.

"We can discuss it privately when we're through here."

The meeting continued in a buzz of indecipherable conversation.

Once they wrapped up, she followed Hope into her office. "Shut the door."

"I'm confused." With a frown, she sat across from her boss. "He fired the entire company?"

"Let's put it this way: we reached a mutual understanding."

She tried to harness her impatience.

"Rafe and I had breakfast with Lucas on Saturday. He informed me he wanted to date you."

Embarrassment heated her entire body. "He said that?"

"And further that he didn't want to work with anyone in the company other than you. Parting ways was the only option at that point."

"Oh my God, I'm so sorry. I don't know what to say."

Hope raised a hand to prevent Wynter from going on. "You did nothing wrong. Lucas is...challenging. In all honesty, I probably should never have signed a contract with him."

"This..." She shook her head. "I can't believe it." Prestige had lost a big account because of her. He wasn't only her first client; he was the only person she handled.

"As for dating him—"

"No. I turned him down."

Hope grinned. "Did you?"

She fought off the desire to explain herself and instead remained quiet as her mind raced.

"There's no policy against it."

"It's complicated."

"Lucas said the same thing."

Did he?

"The choice is entirely yours. You're free to pursue the opportunity, if you'd like. Or tell him to fuck off."

Wynter's mouth fell open. In a million years, she wouldn't have guessed Hope would say that in such a cheery manner. "Have you terminated his contract yet?"

"It's on Miriam's schedule for later this morning."

"Give me a week." Wynter stood, equal measures pissed and determined. She refused to allow Lucas Rutherford to outmaneuver them all.

"Wynter, really—"

"I'm going to fix this." He wanted a wife? She'd get him one. Stat. And ensure he paid the full fee to Prestige while she was at it.

With her shoulders pulled back, Wynter strode to her own office and powered up her computer. This move was hers.

# CHAPTER FOUR

A n hour later, Wynter scrolled to Lucas's contact information. He answered her call on the first ring.

"Ms. Ferguson."

His voice was a gruff, unholy growl that rocketed awareness through her. Damn it. Why did she have to be so responsive to him?

"An unexpected pleasure."

*Is it really?* "This is strictly business."

He was silent for so long that she wondered if he'd hung up. She held the device away from her ear and looked at the screen to be sure they were still connected.

"Of course."

Forcing herself to be professional rather than going weak in the knees, she strode to the window and took in the hustle of midtown a couple of stories below her. "In consultation with Hope, I have two potential matches I'd like to discuss with you."

"Does this mean you'd prefer I didn't cancel my contract?"

Jittery, she paced the room. "I hate for Prestige to have any unhappy clients."

"So you're going to continue as my *personal* handler?"

Wynter forced herself not to respond to the emphasized word. "I'll be working with you, yes."

"In that case, I'm amenable to meeting to discuss your findings."

"How about right now?"

"I do not talk about my business over the phone."

She set her teeth. "I'm happy to send over the profiles."

"Email isn't secure."

Naturally he had no intention of making this easy for her.

"I was disappointed you didn't join me for breakfast on Saturday morning."

Had it mattered to him? Or did he not like the fact she bruised his ego? No doubt His Highness was not accustomed to women standing him up. "I thought you didn't discuss your business over the phone."

"Dinner?"

Frantically she shook her head, even though he couldn't see her.

A donut in hand, Skyler propped her shoulder against the doorjamb and eavesdropped.

"I have a three o'clock coffee appointment available."

With a grin, Skyler took a bite.

"Eleven. My office."

His counter was so quick that he had to have planned it.

"Americano. Large, please. Black."

At every turn, he frustrated her. But she refused to let him know that. "And I'd like you to get me a grande upside down caramel macchiato."

Skyler gave her a thumbs-up.

"Iced or hot?"

"Surprise me."

"I plan to do just that, Ms. Ferguson." With that, he rang off.

She lowered the phone. Instantly her message icon lit up. From Lucas, with his address.

"We've had our share of high-maintenance clients." Skyler had been there long enough to have eaten the entire treat. "But he's in a class by himself."

*That he is.* Wynter's father was a Titan as were most of his friends, so she was familiar with their arrogance. But she'd never met anyone like Lucas.

"Just checking on you. Sorry none of us could take him off your hands on Friday night."

"Everyone's roster was full." And they couldn't have guessed he would ask her out.

"I'd say good luck to you, but from what I overheard, you have it covered."

"I'm not convinced of that." He'd gotten what he wanted. They were meeting in person, on his turf. And she was still his company representative.

After Skyler left, she returned Lucas's text.

*We won't be mixing business with pleasure.*

For more than half an hour, her phone remained silent.

Was he busy? Or keeping her on edge?

*In that case, we'll dispense with the business quickly.*

The man had turned difficult into an art form.

Out of courtesy, she updated her online calendar, letting her colleagues know she'd be out of the office. Hope trusted that her associates would put in the hours required to get the job done.

At the law firm, Wynter's life had been divided into incremental blocks of billable hours. Even though her decision to walk away from the legal profession had annoyed her father, she didn't have any regrets—well, except for the number of pastries she now consumed on a weekly basis. Still, the more flexible schedule allowed her to hit the gym a couple of afternoons a week. Surely that made up for it.

Giving herself twenty extra minutes to arrive at his downtown office and find him a damn Americano, she grabbed her purse, then headed out.

After parking, she discovered there was a coffee shop nearby. The line was ridiculously long, and she was behind schedule when she pushed through the entrance into the skyscraper at 1, International Plaza. As quickly as possible on her heels, she crossed the marble-laden lobby to the bank of elevators and ascended to the thirty-seventh floor.

Inside the door marked Rutherford Consulting was a receptionist wearing a headset. He was an older gentleman with thick, silver hair. When she entered, he greeted her with a smile.

"You must be Ms. Ferguson."

Impressive, made even more charming by his posh British accent.

"Mr. Rutherford apologizes, but he's been unavoidably delayed. He asked that you make yourself comfortable while you wait."

The gentleman pointed to one of the many offices.

She went inside, leaving the door open.

His room was smaller than she expected, and sparse: a credenza, a phone, laptop computer, executive chair, and a battle-scarred desk with nothing on it—well, until she placed his coffee smack dab in the middle.

The lone place for a guest might have been purchased at a military surplus store.

The few shelves on the back wall were empty, and he didn't have a single award or trophy or photograph anywhere in sight. A framed piece of paper hanging above the credenza drew her attention. Curious, she walked toward it.

It appeared to be an article about him, dated a few years ago, speculating that he would soon file bankruptcy.

"Motivation."

With a gasp, she jumped, then slowly turned to face Lucas.

He was holding two drinks, one hot, the other iced.

Smart. No matter which she preferred, she'd be happy. The man didn't play fair.

"The piece was more accurate than I let anyone know."

"Most people surround themselves with mementos of their finest moments and achievements."

"What's the sense in that? Look at it often enough, you might believe your own press." He set her two selections on either side of his Americano. "But those words? They're a reminder of how close I came to losing everything. First thing I see when I walk in here."

Interesting approach.

"Shall we talk?"

Wynter moved so he could take his rightful place behind his desk.

When she sat, her chair tipped sideways, and she had to catch herself so she didn't fall off the seat. "More reminders to keep yourself humble?" Remaining on the cushion would require all her ab strength. "Or to discourage visitors?"

"If there are people in my office, it means both of us are wasting time."

But here she was.

She leaned forward to pick up the iced macchiato. "Do you mind if I give your receptionist the other?"

"I counted on it. You may not like me, but I've seen you interact with others. Of course you wouldn't let a coffee go to waste to make a point."

She hated that he seemed to know so much about her.

"Edmund has a sweet tooth. And it will be perfect with the orange scone I bought him."

Somehow she managed to stand up without losing her balance, she picked up the hot beverage and carried it to Edwin.

"Be sure to come back often." He smiled his thanks.

"Where were we?" Lucas asked when she returned.

"Discussing your potentials." Blazing ahead, she opened her app. "The first is twenty-seven—"

"Too old. Next."

She swallowed her impatience. But before she could continue, his cellphone rang, and he excused himself to answer.

Though she couldn't overhear the person on the other end of the call, he was no doubt speaking to a woman.

"What did you find out?" A few seconds later, he checked his watch. "I'll be there by one."

Then he continued the conversation, all while keeping his gaze on Wynter.

Not allowing herself to be unnerved, she scrolled to the next candidate. Then she took a sip of her coffee.

It was perfect. Creamy, sweet, and cold.

"Love you too."

Wynter blinked. For someone with a heart locked in a deep freeze, his smile and easy expression of affection took her aback.

"I'll let you know what I think." After the call ended, he explained himself. "My sister. She lives in Galveston and asked me to take a look at a building she's considering buying. The owner likes Lyla and thinks it's perfect for her needs. It'll go on the market at the end of the week, and he offered her an opportunity to preview it." He picked up his Americano.

From downtown, the trip could be made in about an

hour, maybe more, depending on traffic. "Let's discuss your second potential so you can get on the road."

"Go with me. Give us an opportunity to talk without interruption."

*What?* A drive to the coast in the middle of a Monday? "What would I do while you looked at the property?"

"Browse shops on the Strand? Have an ice cream cone? Walk on the beach? Have a glass of wine at Pier 21 and watch the barges pass by?"

Damn him. All of those choices sounded much more appealing than being cooped up in the office all day.

"Or you could join me on the tour. Your opinion would be valuable."

She shook her head. "I know nothing about commercial real estate."

"You'd be handy to have around during contract negotiations."

Speechless, she didn't respond.

"I understand you were quite formidable in court."

So he *had* known she was an attorney.

"And out of it too." He grinned. "I need to get going. So if you want to continue trying to talk me into meeting one of the prospects you've found, you'll have to ride along with me."

He was ruthless in the pursuit of what he wanted.

"I'll treat you to dinner on the west end—the Bayview. It's a restaurant that I enjoy, right on the bay. Near the country club, with an excellent view of the sunset."

"I have to work." Even to her own ears, the excuse sounded hollow.

"Because you have so many demanding clients?"

When she didn't respond, he went on.

"There's no reason you can't make phone calls or answer emails from the road."

All true. Besides that, she had plenty of comp time accrued for the weekends she worked. The only thing she would need to do was update her calendar again. And being with him *was* work.

"If you want to go home and change into something more casual, I'll pick you up there."

Giving him her address was stepping into dangerous territory. But the idea of the sand and the surf made her reckless.

A moment later he'd keyed her information into his sleek-looking phone.

"One hour?"

She nodded. That would give her a chance to arrive home, gather a few things, and swap heels for sandals. But it wasn't long enough to rattle her nerves and make her change her mind.

Inside her small condominium not too far from Discovery Green, she hurried to her bedroom and pulled out several different outfits. She rejected a sundress. It might not be warm enough in the evening. Same with a skirt. Then a pair of capris.

The pile growing on top of her bed, she decided on a pair of white pants and a blouse over a T-shirt. Formal enough, but also casual if they did any walking.

Next she hurried to the bathroom and swept the makeup and brushes that she'd used this morning into a drawer.

She had to look in three different places for a ponytail holder. Then, after securing her hair, she wrapped a colorful scarf around it.

*Breathe. This is business. Nothing more.*

Nonetheless she swiped on a coat of the lipstick that she wore when going out with friends.

Woo Me red.

She told herself it wasn't to impress Lucas.

Then she wondered when she'd started lying to herself.

Less than the allotted hour later, she was ready. To burn off nervous energy, she loaded the dishwasher and rinsed the coffeepot.

Good thing she was prompt because he rang her doorbell ten minutes before she expected him.

She answered the summons. He stood on the porch larger than life, in all his masculine glory, the sun toying with the highlights in his raven hair and his aura branding the atmosphere.

Her mouth watered.

Even though he wore slacks and a blazer, there was no way to mistake the fact he truly was American royalty.

She stepped back, and he accepted her unspoken invitation to enter, shutting the door behind him, filling the small entryway.

With a long, lazy smile, he swept his gaze over her. "Everything about you is beautiful."

She gulped. He'd been clear that he wanted to date her, but she needed to keep the boundaries firm. "Mr. Rutherford—"

"Lucas." His correction was light but laced with steel.

Was that his Dom voice?

She shivered as warmth flowed through her. Despite her resolve, that tone packed the power to guarantee her compliance.

"You had to have known what you were doing when you chose that tempting, bright-red color of lipstick."

Quickly she shook her head. "It's the tube that happened to be in my purse."

"You're a terrible liar. You blush when you fib. Was that a detriment in court?"

"Since I always tell the truth, it couldn't have been."

At the preposterous declaration, he laughed.

Earlier when she'd overheard him speaking to his sister, he revealed a whole new side of him. And now, relaxed, he chipped away at her resolve, making him more dangerous than ever.

Wynter's breath froze in her lungs as he leaned toward her to sweep back a loose strand of her hair.

Suddenly remembering their kiss, she yearned for more.

"Shall we?"

Relieved he hadn't done anything more than brush his knuckles down her jawline, she nodded.

His car was a couple of years old, and a brand recognized for reliability over luxury.

"It's better than the one Priscilla and I shared."

"Your name always appears on the top one hundred lists of the world's most wealthy people."

"And I aim to keep it that way."

She waited until they were clear of downtown before pulling out her phone and opening the Prestige app. It was tempting to just forget business, but she had a goal of finding him a bride. "On your profile, you hadn't expressed an age range, yet in your office you said your first match was too old. Did you mean that?"

"No."

If she'd ever met a more confounding man... "Then?"

"She's not you."

"Mr.— " She broke off. "Lucas. We need to be serious."

He looked in her direction. "I am."

Frustrated, she took in a deep breath.

"I was very clear. I'm interested in pursuing you."

"Let's talk about that."

"Go ahead."

"For a million reasons, a relationship between us wouldn't work."

"And you know that how? Did Hope add your profile to her fancy AI database?"

Wynter shook her head. "Of course not."

"So enlighten me."

"We want vastly different things."

"Do we?"

The sun came out from behind some clouds, heating the SUV's interior. Or at least that's the excuse she gave herself to adjust the temperature on her side of the vehicle.

"Children?"

She shifted. How had this become about her? "Yes." Eventually.

"One? Two?"

After seeing how happy her mother and stepfather were with their extended family, she might consider more. "At least."

"Okay. I'm open to negotiation on that."

How were they discussing having hypothetical children together? This couldn't be happening.

"Marriage, I assume, would be part of that?"

When she didn't respond, he went on. "How about a spouse who would support you and encourage you to chase your dreams?"

"That's only the beginning. You'd scoff at what I want."

"Try me."

"The fantasy. A white picket fence and a dog."

"Labrador?"

"That was an easy guess since they're one of the most popular breeds."

"I'll even take turns walking it."

She shook her head. "I want love, Lucas."

"Isn't that an untrustworthy emotion?" This time, he slid her a penetrating glance. "It takes more than that to survive decades. Shared interests? Goals? Similar values. All that can be counted on. But love is fickle. Fall into and back out of it."

"To me, that's the foundation of everything else."

His grip tightened on the steering wheel. "Hope tells me that around the world arranged marriages are the most successful."

"They are."

"Which is what Prestige does, right? Take the emotion out of the decision so people can be rational."

He'd thought this through. "But chemistry matters. It's one of the Three C's."

"Let me be clear about this. I desire you, Wynter, and not in some sweet, romantic way, but with hot-blooded lust."

Scandalized into silence, she stared out the window.

"Tell me you don't feel the same way."

His words had left her reeling.

"That night near the pool, you responded to my kiss."

When she didn't answer, he went on, feeding the tension. "You're attracted to me, and you don't want to be. And I scare the fuck out of you."

Straightening her shoulders in a fake show of confidence, she turned a little to study his profile. His jaw was set in a strong, firm line. His guess was right, and he knew it.

"You're my client, Lucas. Nothing more."

"If that's true, why didn't you join me for breakfast? I've never left a client guessing whether or not I'd show up for a meeting."

The years spent practicing law had taught her to think quickly, but she didn't have an answer to his question. And now she was embarrassed that she hadn't responded.

"As I thought."

A few minutes later, the traffic thinned out, and when they were south of Texas City, the terrain eventually became marshy.

When they passed the first, colorful Galveston sign indicating they were heading over the water, she exhaled.

"My sister tells me this is called the causeway effect."

Grateful for the change of conversation, she looked at him again.

"When you leave the mainland and head onto the island, stress vanishes."

"I think there's something to it." The waves captivated her, mesmerizing her.

"Did you decide what you wanted to do while I look at the property?"

"All of it. I'm happy to tour the building with you. But I also want to shop, enjoy an ice cream cone, and have a glass of wine at the harbor."

"Your wish is my command."

He was willing to do all those things?

Answering her unspoken question, he explained. "We've got all day."

He found parking, and they walked the couple of blocks necessary to meet with the real estate agent.

"Is your sister joining us?"

"No. She looked at the building before she called me, and she's setting up a show this afternoon."

"What does she do?"

"She's a painter who runs an artist's retreat down here. An opportunity to expand her offerings has come up, and this seems like the ideal location. Not just bigger, but room for growth, and she thinks the lighting is better. She wants her big brother's opinion on whether it's an investment or money pit."

"So this would be...what? Studios? Residences?"

"Potentially both. And a retail space, which is something she doesn't have right now."

They turned the corner onto Market Street.

A tall, no-nonsense woman with short blond hair and holding an electronic pad met them inside the door.

"Suzanne. Thanks for doing this."

She nodded. "Not that you gave me a choice."

Lucas introduced Wynter to the real estate agent. "She's been representing our family for twenty years and is an expert in the Galveston market."

The interior needed some work, but the original craftsmanship was evident in many places, from intricate woodwork to the ornate wrought iron detail.

Behind part of the building was a stone-enclosed courtyard.

"This is Lyla's favorite feature. She's suggesting trees, a fountain. Maybe something Zen-inspired. Awnings to filter the sun during the afternoons. And maybe a pergola or gazebo."

Wynter nodded. "I can see why she's excited. This is also a great place for gatherings and showings."

"Lyla said the same thing."

"And it's priced to sell?"

"About twenty to twenty-five dollars a square foot under market value."

"Taking some of the renovation costs into consideration." Wynter grimaced in his direction. "I'm sorry. Am I'm asking too many questions?"

"Not at all. That's why I brought you along."

"Do you have an estimated timeframe for renovations?" he asked Suzanne.

"It's only a guess, as you know, because a contractor would know a lot more than I do."

Lucas nodded.

"And building permits," Suzanne added. "Start date."

"Been through that before."

"I'd say a year. Maybe eighteen months." Then she winced. "Could run a little longer."

Wynter had another question. "Is your sister happy with this location?"

Suzanne answered for him. "It's about a block away from where she'd ideally like to be. But Strand is among the priciest real estate downtown."

"And does that have the best artists' vibe? Or is it too commercial?"

"She also considered that."

They finished up in the main, large, open space. "Can you send me the comps and your recommended offer?"

"You'll have it this afternoon. Let me know as soon as possible. Otherwise Lyla will have to compete with others."

"Maybe end up in a bidding war?" Wynter asked.

"Yes."

They thanked Suzanne for her time, then headed outside.

"I'd suggest we start with that ice cream, but neither of us had lunch."

"And we're having dinner."

"How about appetizers and cocktails at Pier 21?"

"I'm in."

They headed toward the water. Since it was after spring break and before the summer school holidays, the streets weren't packed, though plenty of people enjoyed drinks in front of the Strand's historic shops.

Because it was a beautiful afternoon, before the upcoming oppressive heat, they opted for a table on the patio.

She asked for a rum punch, and he ordered almost all of the appetizers on the menu, along with a white wine.

A dolphin tour blasted its horn, then entered the harbor.

When their beverages arrived, they clinked the rims together, just as a barge slipped by.

"This was a wonderful idea." She took a sip of the killer drink, vowing not to have more than one. Unless she could take a nap on the beach. "I'm not sure why I never think to come down here for a quick getaway. It's such a short trip."

"I wonder the same thing every visit. I understand why my sister settled here."

After the server cleared the dishes and brought the check, they walked back to the Strand for an ice cream. "Only place in the world you can still buy this brand."

She'd heard of it, and with its high butterfat content, the double scoop of praline pecan was even more delicious than she imagined. "This is the stuff of dreams. I'd drive down here just for this."

"I tell Lyla I'm coming to see her, but really I come for the mint chocolate chip."

She laughed.

By unspoken accord, they meandered all the way to one end and then back, window shopping.

They arrived back at the car and drove toward the seawall. Colorful umbrellas and chairs dotted the beach, becoming sparser as they traveled west, out of town.

"I haven't been to this part of the island before."

"Completely different. A charm of its own."

The road widened, and massive, gorgeous homes on stilts lined the Gulf side. "It's a little wilder out here."

"It is." Off to the right, he pointed out a bright pink bird. "Roseate spoonbill."

"How did you know that?"

"Lyla likes to come out here to cleanse her artistic palate. The first time I saw one, I thought it might be a flamingo. She laughed her ass off at my expense."

A smile toyed with Wynter's lips, but she wiped it away.

About five minutes later, he turned right, heading for the bay.

They opted to dine alfresco once more, each feasting on platters of Gulf shrimp. "That's it," she pronounced. "I'll never settle for anything else."

"Sweet, isn't it?" He met her gaze. "Succulent."

He made the word something sensual.

After dinner, he topped off their wineglasses from the bottle they'd ordered, and they walked to the end of the extended pier to watch the sun sink into the bay.

She took out her cell phone and snapped dozens of photos as the colors deepened and intensified.

"Better than being in the office?" Next to her, watching everything she did, he smiled.

"I'd like your version of work."

When they started the drive east, the sky was inky and star studded. Instead of continuing onto the seawall, he turned south and parked on the sand.

"I promised you could do all the things, and that included walking on the beach."

She wasn't sure she'd ever enjoyed an afternoon more. Her high-maintenance client was remarkably hospitable when he was getting his own way.

After kicking off her shoes, she joined him at the water's edge. Though it was still spring, the water was amazingly warm.

The night was perfect, balmy and moonlit. Gentle waves lapped against the shore.

Once they were out of sight of houses, he stopped. "Consider this your fair warning. I'm going to kiss you."

Her heart jumped into her throat.

She shouldn't let him.

He gently cupped her face in his massive palms. The silvery moon made his eyes even darker, and she wasn't sure she'd ever again look up at the night sky without thinking of him.

Though he gave her plenty of opportunity to refuse his advance, she couldn't deny him.

He slanted his mouth over hers. This kiss was different from the one they shared at the hotel, equally sexy, but he was a touch more demanding, as if he wanted much more than her surrender. He wanted her wholehearted response.

When she moaned, silently screaming, *"Yes,"* he pressed deeper into her mouth.

He tasted of the exquisite wine and promise, and his tongue mated with hers. Motions deliberate, he rested his hand on her buttock, holding her in place. Then he began to squeeze, increasing the pressure as he intensified his kiss.

Arousal flooded her. The more he asked for, the more she ached to give.

In that moment, a small lick of pain rocked through her from the bite of his fingers, and she groaned.

She was instantly and totally turned on and hungry for more.

By slow, gentle measures, he eased away, leaving her on a jagged, insistent cliff.

"I know what you want, Wynter." He stood close, his eyes intense, the force of his will engulfing her. "Are you brave enough to ask for it?"

# CHAPTER FIVE

Wynter could blame it on the moonlight or his charm. Or her powerful response to him. Or the wind might have tugged away her resistance, dragging common sense with it. "Yes."

"I'll get us a room."

*Was he afraid she might change her mind if they waited until they returned to Houston?*

To her, that was a legitimate concern. An hour, maybe an hour and a half in the car, was a lot of time to rethink her decision.

Thirty minutes later, they were in the suite of one of Galveston's most luxurious resorts on the top floor, with a room overlooking the Gulf.

Nerves, that had been nowhere to be found earlier, now assailed her.

But then he purposefully crossed the room and gathered her close.

His kiss was gentle.

As she met his thrust with a parry of her own, he groaned.

That she affected him thrilled her.

He moved a hand between her legs and teased her as he tasted her mouth. She'd never been more turned on in her life.

On some level, she expected him to stop, but he didn't. He continued to play with her until she whimpered, silently crying his name.

Her body shook as the climax built.

Oh God.

She had given herself hundreds, perhaps thousands of orgasms, but nothing compared to his confident touch, so much different from her own.

In desperation, she ground herself against him, seeking completion.

And he gave it to her.

The friction he created was enough to drive her to orgasm.

Her entire body shaking, she came. Somehow the kiss ended, and he was there to catch her, and he held onto her until her tiny shudders ceased.

Even when she was breathing normally, he kept her close. "Before we go any farther, we need to talk."

Because of what they'd shared, she guessed where the conversation would lead. Once she'd had a taste of him, he had to have known she'd want more. "I'm hoping you have condoms?"

A smile teased his lips. "I bought a box the night we met."

"You did?"

"I hadn't needed them since my divorce."

Which, she knew, had been at least a couple of years prior. He'd been celibate? Given his stunning good looks and the fact he could have any woman he chose—even without offering anything—the news startled her. "But you were sure of me?"

"No." As he spoke, he massaged her shoulders. "I was hopeful. There's a difference. And you know the option of marriage is on the table."

"Well…" Thinking while he was touching her was almost impossible. "You can remove it. I'm not looking for that."

"Again, I remain eternally hopeful."

"And persistent."

He nodded agreement. "But protection wasn't the only thing I wanted to discuss."

"BDSM?" When he raised an eyebrow, she explained herself. "It's on your intake form."

"It's a beautiful evening. Let's have this discussion on the balcony, shall we?"

It might be easier. Even though she'd brought it up, she had no idea where it would go.

Outside, ships dotted the horizon and palm trees swayed in the breeze.

He adjusted the two chairs so that they angled toward each other rather than the water.

Because it was a Monday night in the offseason, it seemed they had a lot of the hotel to themselves.

"What do you know about BDSM?"

"My best friend is in the lifestyle and attends a club." A little uncomfortable talking about this, even though it was necessary, she shrugged. "We've talked, and we watched a few movies together."

"And you have no experience of your own?"

"No." She tucked escaped strands of hair behind her ear. "From what I understand, not everyone is into everything."

"True. For example, I find it pleasing when my woman does things for me."

She wasn't his woman. Not now, not ever. "I'm not subservient."

"That's not what I'm talking about. Acts of service are an

essential part of any intimate relationship. And it goes both ways."

Wynter recalled the way he'd bought her both a hot and an iced macchiato. And also his smile when he took the first sip of his Americano. His nod of approval had been its own reward.

"I don't expect to live BDSM twenty-four seven, but I like to attend clubs, and I enjoy having scenes with my submissive. And I have certain expectations of compliance during them."

"I'm not sure what that means."

"A partner who is willing to engage fully with the scene, rather than just going through the motions. Surrender. Like you do when I kiss you. Not fighting, but embracing."

His voice, deep and gruffly sexy, sent waves of awareness through her.

"I also believe an exquisite amount of pain enhances pleasure."

"Are you a sadist?" She wrapped her arms around herself, resting her hands protectively on her shoulders.

"Relax, little one." His tone was light. "I don't inflict pain for its own sake."

That was reassuring. *Somewhat.*

"On the beach, when I squeezed your sweet ass, did it hurt?"

"No." She shook her head. "I mean, yes. But you started gently and then gradually dug in harder."

"You whimpered."

She hadn't.

"And moaned. That told me it was at least somewhat pleasurable." Intently he studied her reaction.

"It…" How the hell could she explain something she wasn't sure she understood?

"Turned you on?"

"Yes."

"Communication is the essential key in a successful BDSM relationship. I will always be watching you. Are you smiling or wincing? Are you moving your body toward me, silently asking for more? Or are you tightening your muscles in fear? I will be listening to your words and observing your body language. Your tone reveals a million secrets, even those you'd rather hide. And your breathing reveals your state of mind. Are you relaxed? Scared? And your eyes. Are they filled with terror? Or wide and inviting?"

"All of that."

"And more. I will focus all my senses on you, your pleasure, your safety."

Before today, she couldn't have guessed she'd be having this conversation. By itself, it was erotic.

"Not to say that I won't enjoy making you suffer."

"You've been doing that since the moment we first met."

"Have I?" He seemed supremely unconcerned. "Each of my acts is deliberate, meant to invoke some sort of reaction."

"Congratulations on your success rate."

He grinned. "You're willing to concede that I've unnerved you more than once?"

"You're a master at it."

"In BDSM, everything is about consent."

When he'd touched her, kissed her, he had never done anything she hadn't agreed to first. She took comfort from that.

"It can be withdrawn at any time."

She nodded.

"You know what a safe word is?"

"Yes. It stops play, right?"

"It does. What word do you want to use?"

"How about *red*?"

"Good." He nodded. "And one that means you might need

to slow down, allowing you a chance to gather your words or thoughts? In case you need to talk about something or change the intensity of your experience."

Anna Bella had explained that as well. But Wynter had never pictured herself having that kind of discussion with a Dominant. "Yellow."

"So brave."

His words encouraged her and made her want to explore with him.

"Are there things that terrify you or that you refuse to do?"

"To be honest, I'm not knowledgeable enough to answer that."

"Fair enough. There are a million things to choose from, and we won't do anything that makes you uncomfortable."

"What if I don't like anything we do?"

He quirked his lips. "I'll do my best to ensure that doesn't happen. If you don't have a good experience, neither will I." He studied her. "That promise didn't help."

"No."

"If you hate it, we will immediately stop, and I won't ask you to try again."

Which promised a future that they didn't have.

For a few seconds, he was quiet. "That's what you needed to hear."

When she frowned in confusion, he explained. "You unfolded your arms."

She hadn't even noticed.

"Are you ready to turn yourself over to me, little one?" He stood and extended his hand.

Would her legs support her?

Trembling, she slid her fingers against his. As he helped her up, his grip steadied her.

Once they were inside with the sliding glass door sealed

behind them and the heavy drapes shutting out the world, he released her, took a step back, and then stood in front of her, feet shoulder-width apart, hands commandingly on his hips.

"Within sixty seconds, you're going to be naked, on your knees with your legs spread, exposing your entire body to me."

Something she'd never done for anyone else.

"Do you understand?"

Because she couldn't find her voice, she nodded.

"You have two choices. You can remove your clothes yourself or I can strip them off you. Which do you prefer?"

"You've made me nervous as hell."

"You have no idea how much that statement turns me on."

"That's not comforting."

"No. I didn't mean it to be. In fact, I want you unable to think, frightened, aroused, unsure where one begins and the other ends. Most of all, I want to make sure you have the most unforgettable experience of your life."

Anna Bella had mentioned that her favorite part of BDSM was the mindfuck she went through. Until this moment, Wynter hadn't known what that meant. But now, her mind was spinning.

"You've already wasted most of your time. Take off your scarf for me."

Her fingers were shaking so hard that she fumbled with the knot.

"I see you'll need a little help."

She sucked in a breath as he loosened the silk, then wrapped it around his hand.

After she somehow managed to remove the elastic ponytail holder, he feathered his fingers into her hair, then dropped a gentle kiss on her forehead.

Inhaling deeply, she surrendered to the sensual spell he wove.

"Everything about you is perfect, little one."

She held onto his wrists, feeling the steady beat of his pulse, captivated in him. By him.

"And since you're out of time, I'll decide for you. I'll watch while you remove your clothes. Start with your sandals."

After releasing her grip, she followed his first order.

And it was a calculated one. Barefoot, she was even shorter in front of him. Now he towered over her, making her aware of how much bigger he was.

*Mindfuck* was right.

He returned to his earlier ultramasculine stance. For a moment she pictured him as a pirate standing on the deck of his ship, ready to plunder.

"Blouse and T-shirt, then slacks."

Which left her wearing nothing but her lingerie.

"Stunning. Now the bra."

He couldn't know how difficult this was for her.

Repeatedly she fumbled with the clasp before it gave way.

"You have gorgeous breasts, Wynter. And your nipples are hard already. Despite your trepidation—and maybe because of it—you're starting the slow descent into arousal."

His words had a mesmerizing effect on her, making her forget her embarrassment.

"Now please turn around and bend over."

At least she was faced away from him. That was a small, much appreciated mercy.

"A thong. Excellent. Displays your beautiful, round ass."

Was it possible to be more mortified? Knowing her temporary Dominant, the man who would soon become her first lover, was leisurely studying her almost naked body.

Her knees trembled as she awaited his next command.

"It will look even more stunning when it's red."

She lost her balance, and had to place a hand on the floor so she didn't tip over.

As if pleased, he chuckled. "Next, remove your panties and kneel in front of me."

Wynter wasn't sure she could actually go through with it. But she managed by looking down at the carpet.

"That's perfect. Even better than I imagined. You're a natural." For long moments, he allowed the words to hang between them. Then he spoke again. "Now put your hands behind your neck and look at me."

Unable to help herself, she did as he said, taking in his powerful thighs and trim waist. His features were stern, formidable in a way she'd never seen before. If it weren't for his constant stream of approval, she might gather her clothes and flee.

"Have you ever been spanked before?"

"No…" She hesitated. Was there something she was supposed to call him?

"Lucas is fine. I'm low protocol. Though if you should ever feel compelled, *Sir* is also acceptable."

Until this moment, she would have never even considered it. But being here, on her knees, nude and her body spread open for him, was an alternate reality where the normal rules of life didn't apply.

He crossed to an armchair and made himself comfortable. "Come to me, little one, and drape yourself across my lap."

"What are you going to do?"

"Add to the number of spanks you'll receive for each moment you delay."

"Ah…"

"That's another." When she didn't move, he spoke again. "Now you're up to two. Shall we make it more?"

Frantically shaking her head, she rose. Forcing down her attack of nerves, she hurried to him.

"For that, I'll deduct that second stripe." Approval softened his voice. Then he prompted her. "You may want to express some appreciation."

Anna Bella had never mentioned this part of the mind-fuck. Then again, she had said that every relationship was different. Perhaps she hadn't been forced to express gratitude to her Dominants. "Uhm, thank you."

"Excellent. Now please get into position."

This was strange and awkward, but she did as he said.

Beneath her, the fabric of his slacks scratched her bare skin, and she was even more aware of how powerfully strong his legs were.

"Put your fingertips on the floor." He jostled her forward a little, ensuring she followed orders.

Self-preservation demanded it.

Then he stroked the back of her thighs and her buttocks, before changing his angle so he could tease her pussy.

Because she'd already experienced an orgasm, she was on the edge within seconds.

"This time, I'm going to make you wait."

"That's not fair."

He laughed. "I'll make it worth it."

The fact he stopped his stimulating ministrations was maddening. When she masturbated, she never prolonged the session. She played with herself, then cleaned up her toys and generally went straight to sleep.

Lucas was opening up whole new worlds for her.

He made small, concentric circles on her buttocks. "I'm going to warm you up."

"Meaning?"

"Bring blood flow to the area so none of my spanks leave bruises. There are times, in some relationships and situations, where there might not be a warmup."

Like if she wanted a mark to remember the scene?

She shook her head to banish the wayward, unwelcome thought.

He began to rub, then increased the friction, jiggling her flesh.

"Almost there."

On and on he went for at least another minute before announcing she was ready.

"I'm going to give you five spanks."

"Yes…"

He delivered the first two in rapid succession to her thighs. Before she processed the sting, he teased her clit, making her squirm. Then he slid a finger slightly inside her and used her dampness to provide lubrication as he brought her to a second orgasm.

Screaming and kicking her legs, Wynter came. Never, never had a climax hit her so hard.

She was still shaking when he picked her up and gathered her close. A little dazed, she stayed there, snuggling her cheek against his chest.

His arms were strong, and he stroked her back comfortingly. And the mind-altering events continued. He'd given her a spanking, causing pain, then a powerful completion, ending with reassurance. All with his hands.

"Are you doing okay?"

Using her palm for leverage, she pressed away from him. "That was…unlike anything I imagined." Despite the conversations she'd had with Anna Bella, Wynter had been wholly unprepared for the total turn on, body and mind.

"If you're agreeable, I'm just getting started."

"I…" *Yes.* "There's more?"

He smiled, and there was tenderness in it. "Some scenes last for hours."

"Not sure I could survive that."

"Something we can work up to. Relationship goals."

His words added to her mixed-up emotions. Part of her very much wanted what he said to be true, even though it was impossible.

He carried her to the bed. "On your back, Wynter." Then he removed the scarf from around his wrist and used it to secure her hands above her head. "You comfortable enough?"

"Somewhat nervous."

"I didn't ask that." His grin was wicked. "We've established that terror is good."

Her tummy performed a somersault.

But instead of asking again, he checked the fit himself, ensuring he could slide a finger between her skin and the silk. "I will always check to be sure your circulation isn't cut off."

Now that she was tied up, her breaths came in shallow bursts. Her nipples were harder than ever.

And obviously he noticed.

He straddled her thighs, which further restrained her. Ensnaring her gaze, he captured one of her breasts in a firm grip before bending over to suck the nipple into his mouth. He swirled his tongue around it, torturing it. Then he gently nipped and tugged before soothing away the ache.

Frantically she bucked, unsure what she wanted. Every single thing he did drove her mad.

For a moment he lifted his head, giving her a break. But before she could even speak, he moved on to her other breast.

Ratcheting up the sensations, he pinched her free nipple between his thumb and forefinger.

She was desperate to have him inside her. "Lucas…"

"Not yet."

Everything he did inflamed her further, making her damp. She ached to hold on to him, feel the ripple of his muscles, and the fact he'd tied her hands frustrated her. Right now Lucas was in complete control of her. "I can't take much more."

"You can." He looked at her. "Do it for me?"

His entreaty inspired her to endure anything. How was that even possible?

Long minutes later, he moved off her to trail kisses down her chest, then lower, past her belly.

"Spread your legs."

Nervous, she complied.

"Can you keep them apart? Or do you need me to secure your ankles to the bedframe?"

"I'll…try." She was certain she didn't want to be completely helpless before him. Or did she?

"That's all I ask." He knelt between her legs and licked her pussy.

"Oh my God!"

"Like that?" He spread her labia to give himself greater access to her.

No vibrator on the planet—and she'd tried most of them —had ever rocked her this hard.

Tormenting her, he kept her on edge, then with a chuckle pushed her over it. This—Lucas—was the incarnation of every fantasy.

Perspiration from the physical demands dotted her skin. After he tugged off the restraint, he picked her up and pulled back the bedspread. Then he covered her to ward off her chill.

"I want to make love to you."

She wanted nothing more.

Tired, and a little woozy from everything she'd been through, she turned on her side to watch him undress.

Hell and back. Standing there in his boxer briefs, he was even more sensational than she imagined.

His biceps and leg muscles bore the kind of definition

that came from hours of punishing practice. And his abs…? Heaven help her. He could have walked out of the pages of a fitness magazine. "Damn, Lucas. You're a sexy man."

He grinned, making her glad she'd said something.

Then he removed his underwear, and her mouth fell open. His erect cock was much bigger than she expected. Not just big but…very, very large.

He rolled a condom into place before joining her.

With his mouth on hers, he swept away her worries, kissing her senseless, then lowering his head between her legs and taking care to be sure she was ready for him.

"So slick." But still he continued, bringing her to the knife-edge of another stunning orgasm. "That's it."

Then he positioned himself on top of her, his cockhead at her entrance. Digging his hand into her hair, he kissed her until nothing remained but the sensation of him entering her with slow, methodical movements designed to thrill.

A few seconds later he froze. "Wynter?"

She looked at him.

"You're…you're a virgin?"

Since there was no real reason to answer his question, Wynter pressed her lips together.

"Why didn't you tell me?"

"It's not important."

"The fuck it's not." His vocal cords strained. "And you don't get to decide that."

"I want this, Lucas." She stroked the side of his face. "I want *you.*"

His arms shook from the struggle of holding his weight off her. "Wynter—"

"Make love to me." Deep down, she knew she'd been waiting for someone like him.

"We need to talk."

This moment, she yearned for completion. "Later." He'd

said he would watch all of her reactions to know how she was doing, and now she studied his.

His eyebrows were knitted together, and his internal struggle played out in his eyes. He wanted to have sex with her, and he wanted to be certain she was okay.

She lifted her hips. "Please, Lucas."

"Wynter."

With unaccustomed boldness, she pulled down his head. "Kiss me."

He sank into her, and he captured her small whimper with his mouth.

Then when she shifted, spreading her legs wider and wrapping one of her legs around his to accommodate his length and girth, he took her with longer strokes.

Feminine instinct took over, and her body welcomed him deeper.

As she became wetter, he rode her harder.

Their kiss ended, and she held onto him as the room spun. *"Lucas."*

"Take it, little one."

He possessed so much masculine force, but he constrained it with tenderness.

Tipping back her head, crying out her pleasure, she orgasmed.

When she returned to earth, he changed his tempo, seeking his own release.

God, she loved the feel of him inside her, adored watching the ripple of his muscles. Then he came with a guttural groan.

She held him tight, and he kissed her once more, with meaning.

"We need to talk."

"I was afraid of that."

He eased himself from inside. "Stay here."

She wasn't sure she could move, even if she wanted to.

In all his naked glory, he strode to the bathroom. Water splashed in the sink, and he returned dressed in a robe and carrying another.

He sat on the edge of the mattress and pressed the warm, damp washcloth between her legs. "You were amazing, Wynter. Thank you." He swept her hair back from her face.

Then he helped her to sit up and held the robe for her to shrug into. She knotted the belt around her waist. Then she scooted over so he could climb into the bed next to her.

"That's a hell of a gift to give someone."

She'd never looked at it that way.

"I would have been more thoughtful with you."

"Honestly? I can't imagine it being any more wonderful than it was."

He pulled her against him. "We wouldn't have started with the BDSM."

"That was pretty spectacular too." And she was curious to explore it further. As long as she could do it without opening her heart to him.

"Tell me how that was for you. What did you enjoy? What would you prefer not to do again?"

"I honestly wasn't sure whether or not I'd like BDSM at all. But then…"

"Then?"

"Your words, your voice… They send shivers through me."

Next to her ear, he growled. "This tone?"

Swift and sure, anticipation chased through her.

"I'll give you a little time to recover. How was being restrained?"

She thought about it. "Freeing. That's ironic, isn't it?"

"Not at all. You're able to struggle and let yourself go."

And intuitively she'd know she could trust him.

"Being naked? Kneeling?"

"It was a rush."

He waited while she found the words to express herself.

"It changes things, you know? We were talking, and then when I undressed, something shifted inside me, and there was no doubt that we were involved in a scene."

"A dividing line between the real world and an even better one?"

Where emotion and sensation blurred, pain was pleasure. "That's a good way to put it."

"You were an exquisite sub."

Everything they'd shared caught up to her, and she yawned.

He lay down, then tugged her into place next to him. Behind her, his body was rock solid, and his protection was absolute.

"You're mine, Wynter."

Smiling, she wiggled around until she was more comfortable.

"I don't think you realize how serious I am. But I promise you, you'll find out."

# CHAPTER SIX

After slipping from the bed before sunrise, Lucas tucked the covers around Wynter's shoulders. She gave a soft smile but didn't open her eyes as she drifted back to sleep.

For a moment he stood there, unmoving, looking at her, adoring the way her blonde hair spilled across the pillow.

The first time they'd met and verbally sparred, he'd known she was different—not at all intimidated by his personality or impressed by his accomplishments. She'd called him out for essentially being an asshole. Although she might not have used that word, there'd been no doubt about her meaning. He grinned at the memory. That she was both beautiful and intelligent was an added delight.

And then last night...

*Fuck.*

Her innocence had blown his mind.

In business, Lucas was recognized for being perceptive, seeing through bullshit to get to the bottom line. The way she'd reacted to his unspoken command to come to him at the mixer had convinced him she'd be receptive to BDSM. Yet he hadn't known she was a goddamn innocent.

The air conditioner kicked on, somewhat taming the hard-on he got every time he looked at her or even thought of her.

He crossed into the bathroom to take a shower, letting the hot, pulsing spray pound the back of his neck.

Thoughts returned to the sexy submissive in the bed.

If he had realized the truth about her, would he have still pursued her?

He wiped water droplets from his face. *Absolutely yes*. Out of all men, she'd bestowed that honor on *him*, and that deepened his resolve to claim her forever.

Lucas was her first. And he sure as hell intended to be her last.

Memories of her moans, and the sweetness of her surrender, had hardened his dick.

A storm around three had awakened them both, and he'd made love to her a second time. It had been less intense yet created a deeper connection, and she'd crawled on top of him and rode him to completion.

She was his.

If she thought he was kidding about that last night, she was wrong.

And starting today, she'd find out just how serious he was.

After he got himself off, he toweled dry, then pulled on his slacks and shirt.

Wynter was curled on her side, sleeping deeply when he returned to their suite. Despite an orgasm less than five minutes before, he was ready again. Maybe going commando hadn't been a good idea.

Quietly he left the room in search of coffee. The miniature machine in the room would only spit out enough caffeine to piss him off. Today, after last night's lack of sleep, called for extra-large cups.

The kiosk was small, and he was third in line, giving him time to check his phone and learn that Lyla had submitted an offer on the building and was going out of her mind while she waited for a call from her real estate agent.

When it was his turn, he ordered himself an Americano and the biggest size macchiato for her. Then he added a couple of sweet pastries and breakfast burritos to their bill.

No matter what she was hungry for, he had her covered.

When he entered the room, she blinked awake. "The bed was cold without you."

"A coffee will warm you up." After setting things down on a table, he carried her cup to her.

With a sleepy sigh, she sat up, dragging the covers with her.

When he extended his offering, she bravely popped out one hand. "Would you like your robe?"

"Or for you to get back in here with me."

"That might have been the best invitation I've ever had."

As he removed his clothes, she took a small sip. "You remembered."

"I listen to every word you say. And I guessed that the first coffee of the day should be hot and not cold."

"You were right." She wiggled against the headboard to get more comfortable.

"Hungry."

Seductively she drew her eyebrows together. "What do you have in mind?"

Who was this vixen? "I think we're on the same page."

With a giggle, she placed her cup on the nightstand. He threw the covers back and grabbed her ankle to drag him toward her.

Gasping, laughing, she met his gaze. And her expression

changed, becoming much more serious. Her stunning blue eyes widened, and her lips softly parted. My God, had she slipped into a submissive mindset just from the way he looked at her?

He'd had no idea a woman so perfect for him actually existed. "Spread your legs, little one." When she did as he said, he nudged her ankles farther apart.

"You're making me nervous."

"Am I?"

"I'm unsure what to expect. What you're planning to do." Her nipples hardened, and her chest rose and fell rapidly. "Or if it will hurt."

"Oh it will. I guarantee it."

Instantly she brought her thighs together.

"Don't test me, Wynter."

"I…"

"You've trusted me so far."

Her sky-blue eyes were wide, expressive, honest. In their depths, he read her struggle and her overwhelming desire to please him.

Arms folded, with infinite patience, he waited her out.

Hesitantly, as if calling on all of her inner resolve, she crawled back into the position he'd requested.

"Your obedience is beautiful."

He stroked her clit, delighted to discover her pussy was already damp. He couldn't ask for anything more in the perfect wife.

For a few moments, until she closed her eyes and relaxed, he played with her, taking care to bring her to the brink of an orgasm. Then he stopped and leaned forward to lick her.

"Lucas!" She thrashed.

Instantly he ceased what he was doing and gave her a light tap.

As her body froze, she yelped. Then seconds later, he sucked away the hurt.

"Oh. Oh… My…"

"Tell me."

"I can't. That's…" In silent invitation, she lifted her hips.

He seized the opportunity to spank again, this time with three fingers, being sure his touch stung.

*"Fuck."*

He pressed a palm against her belly, ensuring they stayed physically connected through the process. "Use a safe word if you need it."

"Hell no."

He grinned. For her honesty, he rewarded her with an orgasm.

Then, when she spread her legs even wider, he spanked her pretty little cunt in earnest, with quick, sharp slaps.

She was panting, crying his name when he went down on her, finger-fucking her as he tormented her clit with his tongue.

When she grabbed his hair, begging to come, he penetrated her with a second, and then a third finger.

Her body became rigid. "Yes. I need…"

And he didn't want her to climax again so quickly. To prevent that, he lifted his head. In protest, she moaned.

"Don't worry. We're not done. You're about ready for me." *Ready?* Drenched was more like it. Hot and willing for him and him alone. So absolutely perfect. "Please get on your hands and knees."

Lucas helped her to sit up. Then he kissed her lips. "Taste yourself on me."

His precious submissive sucked in a sharp breath.

"Honey. The nectar of desire." Then he pressed his damp fingers against her mouth. "I could lick your sweetness all day long."

While she situated herself in the middle of the bed, he rolled a condom down his cock. Maybe, until they agreed to start a family, he should have the protection autodelivered to his home. They were going to need them.

He moved in behind her and trailed his finger down her spine. "Are you doing okay?"

"My pussy is on fire."

"In a good way?"

"Maddening." She nodded.

With luck, the sting would last through the day, a reminder of his dominance after they arrived back in Houston.

He made certain she was still damp before pressing his demanding cock against her.

"Oh…"

"Tender?"

"Somewhat. But I need to have you inside me."

He gave her right ass cheek a couple of swats, and she swayed from side to side. Her breasts moved, and he reached beneath her to capture one and squeeze the tip.

"You're just… I never guessed it could be like this."

Gritting his back teeth so he could limit the depth of his strokes, he entered her. Testosterone urged him to take her hard, claiming her in a way that left his mark on her.

But his civilized side demanded restraint.

"This is…intense."

For him as well. Her hot pussy closed around him, the fit tight like a sheath. It was as if they were meant to be together.

"So deep. *Lucas!*"

He placed his hands on her hips, holding him steady while he filled her again and again.

"You're…" Her words were lost in a tumble of moans. "I had… Wow." Then she whimpered as she climaxed.

Elated by her lack of inhabitation and how wet she was, he unleashed a fraction of his control.

When she climaxed a second time, the contraction of her internal muscles drove his orgasm.

Digging his fingers into her, he groaned as he came, even harder than before.

Then, even when he was spent, he held onto her much longer than necessary, because he was reluctant to end their morning and return to reality.

Eventually she shifted her weight. He withdrew, then gave her butt a little slap.

With a yelp, she collapsed onto the bed.

"I'll get you a washcloth."

She rolled over to study him. "I'm not sure how this is all supposed to go, but I think you're spoiling me."

"There's plenty more to look forward to."

"Lucas—"

"Your coffee is getting cold." Without waiting for a response, he crossed to the bathroom.

When he returned, she was popping a bite of pastry into her mouth. "When are we heading back?"

"I'm in no hurry. You?"

"I'd like to get to the office by ten. Which means I need to be home by nine, at the latest."

He glanced at the clock on the nightstand. Taking traffic into account, that gave them less than forty-five minutes. Not long enough for the shower together that he was going to suggest.

Fortunately she was showered and ready to go in half an hour, which left her time for a second round of coffee while the valet brought the vehicle around.

The sun was shining brightly when they joined the line of vehicles accelerating onto the causeway.

"I think I'd rather be coming to Galveston than leaving it."

He nodded agreement.

For the first part of the drive, she was quiet.

"What's on your mind?"

"Nothing." Cup in hand, she looked at him. "And everything."

"Such as…?"

"I enjoyed that."

"So much more to explore."

"We're still working together, and I have a job to do."

*For now.* "You could marry me. Let Prestige keep my full payment, and you get to celebrate because your first client was a complete success."

"Is there a part of *no* that you don't understand?"

"All of it."

In exasperation, she shook her head.

His phone rang with a call from Edwin. He excused himself to answer it.

While they spoke about the day's schedule, she opened her work app. He caught sight of a picture of himself.

*"Handsome fellow,"* he mouthed.

In a whisper, she answered him. "And also humble."

As they approached the metro area, the highway backed up, and he concentrated on navigating rush hour.

They arrived at her house a couple of minutes earlier than he anticipated.

"I…" She trailed off. "Thank you for a wonderful time."

"Dinner tonight?"

"I should catch up on the things I didn't do last night." She dropped her phone into her purse. "There's a mixer on Friday. Four to six at the Bluewater Bistro on Westheimer. Should I contact Edwin to add it to your calendar?"

He shook his head. "I won't miss an opportunity to be with you, Wynter."

"Even if I'm searching for your future wife?"

"Even if." Lucas cut the car engine and jogged around the front of the vehicle to walk her to the porch.

"You don't need to be such a gentleman."

Once she turned the knob, he followed her inside her small, cluttered condo. Her place was much different than his, and he liked its coziness.

He closed the door behind them, then backed her against it. "There was nothing gentlemanly in my intent."

"Lucas…" Her pretty eyes widened as he leaned in toward her.

Her earlier words had been carefully calculated to build an emotional wall between them. Every brick she'd placed, he'd rip out.

He kissed her hard like he'd been wanting to, plundering and possessing as he simultaneously inserted a hand between her legs to stroke her pussy.

Before she could come, he stopped what he was doing and stepped back, leaving her breathless, her palm to her chest.

"I will see you soon, Wynter. And in the meantime, don't masturbate." He dug a hand into her long hair. "You'll confess it to me if you do."

She shook her head, tugging against the strands he held and making her wince.

"Shall we bet, little one?"

Her mouth parted a fraction of an inch.

"Think of me as you plan our wedding." Gently he unfisted her hair, then left the house, planning his next move.

She might not like it. He couldn't say he cared.

Wynter joined Hope and the rest of the Prestige associates in the corner of a gorgeous patio at a popular midtown restaurant. Since it was four o'clock on Friday and presumably people would have dinner later, the chef had arranged for light appetizers, and each attendee would receive two drink coupons upon check in.

"Miriam, what's our final count on guests?"

"About fifty."

Hope nodded. "I'll have three clients here."

Tony adjusted his tie with the bright green palm trees on it. "Two for me."

"Three." Skyler responded after a quick dash to the dessert tray for a brownie.

"And Wynter?"

"I was hoping Anika would be here, but she's tied up." In a show of faith, Hope had given Wynter a second client. "As for Lucas…" She sighed. Though they hadn't seen each other since Galveston, he'd kept her on edge.

Every day he asked if she'd had an orgasm and reminded her not to sneak one without permission. And he promised he'd make it worth her while when they went out next.

Because of his mindfucks, sleep had been an elusive companion. He haunted her dreams as well as her fantasies.

"As for Lucas…?" Hope prompted.

"Sorry." The man was always in her thoughts, distracting her. "He didn't RSVP." But he also hadn't sent his regrets.

"Want one of my drink coupons?" Skyler grinned, extending a red ticket toward Wynter.

She laughed. "Anyone else have extra?"

Tonight's mixer was scheduled to last for two hours. These events were less formal than meet and greets. The guests were people who Hope had met at various functions but who had not hired Prestige. Miriam and the company's part-timers prescreened everyone in attendance to be sure there weren't any unpleasant surprises.

Because she had no specific clients here tonight, Wynter's job was to mingle, facilitate introductions, lookout for issues, and backup her teammates.

Now if she could just stop looking toward the entrance to see if Lucas had arrived...not that she needed to check. When it came to him, all of her senses lived on hyperalert, and her nerve endings flared to life when he was near.

Most of the guests had left, and Hope was wrapping up with her last client when the tiny hairs on the back of Wynter's neck stirred. She froze. Then when her heart rate was under control, she turned to face the man who dominated her body with the same force he did her brain.

Lucas's shoulders were propped against the wall with his arms folded

Tonight he was more formal than ever in a well-tailored business suit. Though many women interestedly looked in his direction and a couple of conversations stopped, his gaze was focused on Wynter and only her.

Without him using a single gesture or speaking her name, she went to him, drawn as surely as a moth embracing its demise as it fluttered toward a flame.

"I see my match is still here."

Wishing the heat that rushed to her cheeks wasn't betraying her, she looked at him. "For it to be a match, both people have to agree."

"That's right." He grinned, and there was a trace of mockery on his face. "Monday night proved we have no chemistry."

Memories of their kisses, including the most intimate kind, clawed at her again.

"I didn't want you driving home alone this late."

It was barely six, almost two hours before it would be dark.

"Another part of marriage is having someone to count on, share life's burdens."

Right now that sounded delicious.

"I also assume you're hungry."

"Thanks, but I have leftovers in the fridge."

"I'll take that as a yes, you would enjoy an actual meal."

"We're not dating." Did he hear any of her protests?

"I took the liberty of making us reservations. Our table is ready if you are."

With a smile, Hope approached, interrupting the beginning of their argument. "Lucas. We're so very glad you made it."

"How are you, Hope? Looks like another successful event. Congratulations."

They hugged.

"However nice it is to see you, I came to collect Wynter."

Exasperated, she closed her eyes. It was one thing for him to have told Hope that he wanted Wynter, but to make a claim so publicly was beyond the beyond.

"You should have used that drink ticket when you had the chance." Skyler grinned as she joined the small group.

"I don't believe we've had the pleasure." The smile he gave Skyler oozed with charm. "Lucas Rutherford."

"A…" Skyler seemed to lose track of what she was saying, and for a moment she just stared at the hand he offered before accepting. "I, uhm… Hello."

Wynter had never known her associate to be flustered by anything or anybody. After all, she worked with the rich and infamous every day. "Skyler is my teammate."

"I enjoy meeting Wynter's coworkers." His manners, when he chose to use them, were irresistible. "Now if you'll excuse us, I have a table waiting."

"Lucas—"

His look—frost and steel—shut her up.

While Hope and Lucas said goodbye, Skyler leaned over to Wynter and whispered, "Swoon and a half."

With a small laugh, Wynter shook her head.

Possessively he touched her lower back. "Shall we?"

Together they moved toward the door.

As they exited, she overheard Skyler once more. *"Dammmn."*

The table he'd secured was tucked away in an alcove, away from everyone else. Conversation, laughter, and libations flowed all around them.

"It's my first time here."

"The menu is extensive. Including Gulf shrimp."

She put down the menu she'd been holding. "You remembered."

"Every single word you've said. Every detail. Every nuance."

If she wasn't so on guard, she might be tempted to fall for him. He had all the right words and the actions to back them up.

Their server stopped by for their drink orders. Wynter opted for a rum punch, while he selected a whiskey. "The same brand you ordered at the meet and greet. Bonds."

"Impressive. Do you do that for all your clients?"

"Until recently, you were the only one."

"You wound me, fair lady."

Wynter laughed. Someone needed to. Otherwise he'd become too accustomed to women fawning all over him.

"Tell me about your new client."

"She's an executive at a tech company. I had Hope run the program to see if you two were a match." She paused. "Only came back at fifty percent."

"Because?"

"You're not tall enough."

As if realizing she'd made that up, he grinned.

The truth was, Anika had specified that she wanted a husband who shared her religion. If they didn't find a match within a month or two, Hope would have to consider a gentleman who lived out of state or even overseas. If that were the case, Wynter would accompany Anika on any such trip.

"How did your evening go?"

"Better than expected. Hope has done a great job of raising the company's profile." A couple of clients had met people they were interested in talking to. And four of their guests had paired up. "Not everyone is as particular as you are."

"Discerning is the word I prefer."

She laughed.

"I am perhaps Prestige's least difficult client ever."

"First woman I saw, I wanted. No need to go through a tedious process of elimination."

Saving her from a reply, their server returned with their beverages and took their order.

He was right about the quality of the food at the Blue-water Bistro. The ambience was equally as wonderful.

"What did your sister decide about the property?"

"She put in an offer. The seller rejected it, so she countered. They'll be closing within ten days."

"That's impressive."

"You'll have to go to her grand opening with me."

Which could be two years in the future. Her breath hitched. By then, he'd be married, and maybe he'd even have a child on the way.

After dinner, they passed on dessert but said yes to coffee.

Lucas drew his cup toward him.

She opened her mouth but changed her mind.

"There's something you want to know."

"I'm being nosy."

"You have a right to be. As I've mentioned before, communication is crucial."

"You've told me about your first wife. Priscilla?"

"Good memory."

"And that something happened that you won't ever forgive with your second wife. I'm sorry, I don't recall her name."

"Ileana."

She took a drink of her strong coffee and waited for him to continue, wondering if he would.

A tiny pulse ticked in his temple. "We celebrated when she got pregnant."

His words were unexpected.

"And mourned when she miscarried." His eyes darkened. With pain?

"That's horrible. I'm so sorry."

"It turns out, it wasn't my baby."

She shivered. The ice in his tone dropped the room temperature by ten degrees.

"I gave her my heart. And she ground it beneath her heel."

Wynter shook her head, unable to believe such treachery was possible.

"Our relationship was fake from the beginning. She and her boyfriend were using me to finance their own lives together. I was an idiot—besotted enough not to see it."

His words proved to her that he would never open his heart again.

Moments later his phone rang, and she was grateful for the interruption.

He checked the screen. "Lyla." With a swipe of his finger, he sent the call to voice mail. "We've already talked half a dozen times today."

The server returned with the bill, and Lucas took care of it.

Before they could leave the table, his phone rang for the second time.

"It must be important."

"What we were talking about matters."

Wynter shook her head. "We'll pick this up in the future. If there's anything more to say." Since his eyebrows were still knitted together in indecision, she nodded. "Really."

"I'll make it quick." He answered. "I'm at dinner. What's up?"

Even from across the table, the panic in Lyla's voice was evident.

Lucas scowled. "Take a breath, and slow down."

After Lyla spoke again, his spine stiffened, and his face paled. He checked his watch. "I'll be there in twenty minutes. You be safe. No driving like a bat of hell."

He ended the call and met her gaze. "My dad... He was taken by ambulance to the hospital."

"I hope everything's going to be okay."

"Could be a stroke."

"How can I help? Is there anything you need?"

"You to accept my apology for cutting our evening short."

"Oh God, no. Not at all." She shook her head. "You need to go."

"Let me drive you home."

"Lucas, no. I mean it. If you hadn't shown up tonight, you wouldn't have been worried about me."

"Not true. But we can add that to the topics we will continue to discuss."

Though his vehicle arrived first, he waited for the valet to return with hers.

He kissed her long and deep, reigniting the flames she'd hoped had been extinguished by their time apart.

Though she'd tried her hardest to keep her emotional distance from him, she wanted to be there for him.

Once she slid behind the wheel, he leaned in close. "I'll call you."

She nodded.

"I won't forget the plans I had to paddle your sexy, tempting little ass this evening."

# CHAPTER SEVEN

"Wynter?"

At the sound of Hope's voice, accompanied by a light knocking on the door frame, Wynter looked up from her computer where she was studying the most recent addition to her client roster. After removing the ear buds that she used to keep the background chatter at bay, she smiled. "Sorry. I didn't hear you."

"When you're free, I'd like to talk to you for a couple of minutes."

"Sure." She frowned. "Is everything okay?"

Skyler's arrival at work interrupted their conversation. "I'm hearing wedding bells for Larissa and Paul! It's a great way to start a Tuesday!" She lifted the white box that she held. "I figured this celebration calls for a cake. Bonus time! Cha-ching!"

Wynter shook her head. Every success called for a confection, and as did each defeat.

"Congratulations! I wondered if he'd actually get around to popping the question."

"He was almost at the end of his contract." She grinned.

"Maybe discussion about the renewal terms scared the crap out of him."

Hope laughed. "Whatever works."

"Brilliant strategy."

"Let me go cut this thing, and then you can all join me and continue telling me what a great job I did." Skyler sashayed toward the conference room.

"She's good." Wynter still had a lot to learn about how the business worked.

"Sometimes love needs a little nudge."

Could be true. Which might be why some of their clients were willing to pay top-tier fees. Having an advocate mattered.

Somewhere in the distance, above the sound of a ringing phone, Tony's voice reached her. "I don't eat sweets."

"Let me grab a cup of coffee and see if I'm better able to stay away from the cake than Tony is. Shall we meet in about ten minutes?"

"Sounds good." Since she'd already had three cups of mocha and knowing the only way to resist temptation was to avoid it, Wynter opted to continue scanning her new client's file. The woman would be stopping by the office tomorrow in order to meet with Wynter—to be sure they had synergy— before Friday evening's mixer.

With her expectations, this promised to be a difficult assignment. But Hope and the computer had come up with three potentials with a match probability of over eighty percent. Wynter didn't have long enough to study any of Gwendolyn's matches, so she decided to look at those after her meeting.

Instead she straightened her desk, which left her too much time to think.

Since she'd seen him last, Wynter had received two text messages from Lucas. The first was on Saturday night, letting her know his sister had arrived and was planning to stay with him for a couple of days.

The second was Sunday afternoon. His father was stable but would remain in the hospital another twenty-four hours. Because of the prognosis, Lucas planned to return to work on Monday. He added he hoped she was doing well and looked forward to seeing her soon.

Which was another temptation she absolutely had to avoid.

Coffee in hand, Hope passed Wynter's office. "I'm ready for you anytime."

Wynter followed.

"Close the door."

Puzzled, frowning in concern, she did so. "Did I do something wrong?"

"Not at all. Sorry if I alarmed you." Hope shook her head. "I didn't want to mention it in front of the team or take you by surprise."

Then she turned her notebook computer toward Wynter.

"What am I looking at?"

Hope didn't answer.

"An intake questionnaire?"

"You'll want to read it."

Julianna was five foot seven, athletic, and enjoyed running and working out. She owned an international recruiting firm, focusing on the tech industry's highest-priced employees. Last fall, she'd been named as one of Houston's most powerful women.

Her wants included marriage and a child. Two was an option.

She was experienced in BDSM, but it was for stress-relief only. If her husband went to a club, that was fine, as long as it was not in the metro area.

To Wynter, every word was a dagger.

The only thing on Julianna's absolute no list? Love. Her words were clear: *It's a messy, useless emotion.*

Her hand trembling on the mouse, Wynter continued to scroll until she reached the possible match section.

Lucas's name was bolded.

"The match is a hundred percent, Wynter."

Stunned, unable to thread two thoughts together, she sat back.

The news should have delighted her. After all, maybe then she could be the one bringing cake to celebrate a cha-ching worthy bonus.

"I'll let you decide what you want to do about this. How we handle it is up to you. I can send it over or talk to him, if you prefer." Her unspoken words clung to the air.

As his handler, it was her obligation to pass along the information.

Which was exactly what she wanted to do. Wasn't it?

Since she'd taken him on, her focus had been on finding him the mother of his children. He'd get the wedding he desired, and he'd be a satisfied client.

"I'll give you a minute." Hope left, quietly closing the door behind her.

Wynter continued to stare at the screen until her eyes blurred.

Foolishly she'd believed that she could sleep with him, scene with him, without involving her heart.

The lump of emotion clogging her throat told her otherwise.

She'd made a monumental mistake.

Then, with a resolved sigh, she straightened her spine. She knew what she had to do. No matter how difficult.

Standing, she closed the lid of the laptop and picked up her phone.

Though she didn't pick up an Americano for Lucas, Wynter did buy a scone for Edwin before riding the elevator to Rutherford

"Morning, Ms. Ferguson." He removed his headset. "You're a godsend." He rolled his eyes heavenward, and with his accent, he was completely charming. "I'm afraid I didn't have time for breakfast, which means I shall enjoy every bite."

In that case, she was glad she'd put aside her tumultuous emotions and think about others.

"Mr. Rutherford is expecting you, though I wouldn't mind keeping you to myself for a bit longer."

The exchange with Edwin had given her a momentary respite from the upcoming unpleasant meeting with his boss.

"Go on in. He'll be happy to see you."

She doubted that.

After a quick knock, afraid of losing her courage, she entered his office.

He looked up and met her gaze.

Tiny lines were grooved next to his gray eyes. Stress from what he'd been dealing with?

Still, he was shockingly handsome. His white dress shirt was open at the throat, and he'd turned back his sleeves to expose his forearms. "You're a beautiful sight, little one. I've missed you."

God help her. The sound of his rough voice, combined with the way he raked his gaze down her body, her, sent skitters down her spine. She gave herself a mental shake.

"I'm glad you're here. Did you decide you couldn't wait any longer for me to paddle your sexy, tempting little ass?"

She craved him and his touch so much that she ached. To

protect herself, she had to harden her heart, exactly like he had done since his divorce from Ileana.

Remembering how dangerous the guest chair was, she precariously perched on the edge. "How are things with your dad?"

At her change of subject, he scowled.

"Is he still in the hospital?"

"He went home yesterday." Drumming his fingers on his desk, he studied her. "My mother will be back from Italy tomorrow, so my sister will be leaving then."

"Oh. I didn't realize your mom wasn't in the country."

"His stroke didn't seem to be a life-or-death situation. So she opted to continue her baking retreat as scheduled."

The calmness with which he delivered the words made her reel. It was as if no one in his family expected Mrs. Rutherford to interrupt her vacation.

Now she understood him on an even deeper level. He'd seen disinterest modeled in his parents' relationship. For his whole life? No doubt Lucas's behavior was more than a result of the disastrous marriage to Ileana.

Thank God Wynter's mother hadn't been willing to accept her father's chilly attitude. For the first few years of her life, Wynter'd grown up much the same way as Lucas had. But the joy her mom found once she got out of the relationship had been contagious. The laughter in the household rewired Wynter's expectations of what happiness looked like.

The two of them did everything together, were there for each other, no matter what. Wynter couldn't imagine her mother staying overseas if something happened to her husband.

"Now that pleasantries are out of the way, and you've been polite..." He leaned forward again, lancing her with his intensity. "Why are you here, Wynter?"

She needed to get this over with as quickly as possible. "I know you like to discuss your personal business in private."

"Go on."

With a sigh, struggling to hold back her emotions, she pulled out her phone, opened the app, and slid the device across to him. "I'm here to introduce you to Julianna."

"She's attractive."

"Not too tall. Not too old."

"And?"

"Lucas, this doesn't happen often. Julianna is a hundred percent match for you. A marriage has an extraordinary chance of success."

He gave the phone a slight shove, sending it back in her direction.

"I'm happy to set up a meeting." Did he see her lie and how much the words cost her?

"Not interested."

"Not...?" She blinked.

"We need to stop this goddam charade. It's you, Wynter. You're the only one I want."

"You want to stop the charade? Fine." She cloaked herself in the same energy she'd called on at the meet and greet. "We are not a match. While you're Prestige's client, it's my job to find you a wife. If she's not satisfactory, I'll keep searching."

"Cancel my contract. I don't care how much the fee is. Get that bullshit out of the way. I want you, and I intend to marry you."

Frantically she shook her head. Then she stood. "This is goodbye, Mr. Rutherford."

She made it all the way across the room before he caught up to her and put a hand on both the door and the frame to prevent her from escaping.

Drinking in ragged breaths, she turned toward him.

He was so close. His spicy, masculine scent engulfed her. His face was all hard angles, set in determined lines.

"Don't do this to us, little one. What we have is perfect."

"No." Frantically, desperately, she shook her head. "It's not. Can't you see?" She lifted her hand to put it on his chest but changed her mind. She didn't dare allow herself to touch him. "If I give you what you want, you win. And what do I get?" Not waiting for a response, she rushed on. "A lifetime of hurt."

That little tick in his temple became a harsh throb. "That's a fucking lie and you know it. I'm offering you the world. Support and security until the end of time."

"But you're denying me the thing I won't live without. Your only nonnegotiable."

"Wynter—"

"You wondered why I'd kept my virginity? I wasn't interested in investing time with someone I wasn't in love with." Needing to get this out, she rushed on. "You may not think you're capable of it. But I've seen it with your sister, and in the tenderness you've shown me. Like you, I won't settle. I deserve a match that's one hundred percent right *for me.*" She choked on a sob. "Step aside, Mr. Rutherford."

With his famous resolve, or maybe obstinance, he remained where he was.

Her eyes burning with unshed tears, she looked up at him. Through her pain, she uttered the one word that would make this whole thing stop and allow her to protect her shattering heart. *"Red."*

# CHAPTER EIGHT

"Well you're in a fucking morose mood."

Over a glass of whiskey at one of the Sterling's Uptown bars, Lucas met Rafe's gaze.

"Did you even hear a single thing I said?"

He shook his head. "What?"

"You've been here ten minutes without saying a word."

"Sorry, man. It's been a fucked-up few days." The worst in years.

"Assuming so. Which is why I called. Eleven times."

Lucas winced. "Eleven?"

"Maybe twelve. But who's counting?"

*Who indeed?*

Rafe lapsed into silence again, giving Lucas a chance to sift through his thoughts. Then, when the server asked if they were ready for a second drink, Rafe spoke up. "Are we going to sit here and get smashed on this spectacular bottle of single malt?"

That might have been the best fucking idea Lucas had heard all week.

"Another round. Thanks." After Rafe nodded, the server

left. "At least I have a chance to purchase it at wholesale prices."

"The benefits of being friends with Bonds."

"Benefits? You're kidding, right? Man's deep into my pockets."

Jolted from his musings, Lucas focused on his friend. "Any news on that front?"

"Evidently he's waiting to hear from the lone holdout on the second round of funding."

Which meant Rutherford Consulting. Failing that, Bonds would happily dig his fingers into Lucas's bank account. Anything for the genius to have his latest bauble: his very own movie studio. GeniusWorks, or something like that. But his preference was for the company to invest. He was no fool. Bonds wanted someone to help set up the operations so he didn't have to bother. And since Lucas had years of experience in that area, Bonds wanted to lean on his friend.

Which explained the New Year's Eve extravaganza.

Even for Bonds, emerging from a helicopter on the *Stargazer's* deck had been a hell of an entrance.

Cheeky bastard had glad-handed everyone, smiled as he fished for money, then asked his charming pilot, Svetlana, to ferry him back to the airport so the *Tornado*, his plane, could get him to Los Angeles for a star-studded party.

"What's holding you back?"

"Risk assessment." Lucas had spent a lot of hours studying Bonds's business plan. Not that he'd needed to. There wasn't a lot there besides Julien's grandiose imaginings and blue-sky conjectures.

"Could make you billions."

"And the man could lose it all. I'd like to see him put down at least a good-faith token."

*"What?"* Rafe scoffed. "Bonds spend his own money?"

"Absurd request." On the other hand, the man was a bona

fide expert at turning ideas into cash. His company was the most valuable in the world. "I promised him an answer by the end of the month." From what he'd heard, Bonds had already started assembling a team. Which Lucas hoped he didn't have to disassemble if he joined the project. *Scandalicious* reported last week that Bonds had been seen meeting with a director in Hollywood. The accompanying picture was so grainy it was difficult to determine if the gossip was accurate. Most likely was, though. When the genius latched on to an idea, he relentlessly pursued it. Consequences be damned.

"Assuming that investing in Bonds hasn't been keeping you up all night…"

"Haven't lost a minute of sleep over him."

"And your dad?"

"On his way to a full recovery." He shrugged. "Or not. We're told a lot depends on whether he follows doctors' orders, therapy and such."

"What's your guess?"

He had no idea.

For decades, Lawrence had ruled Rutherford Enterprises with an iron fist. Now, for the first time, he seemed weary, as if all energy and the will to fight had vanished.

He'd always decreed that Lucas would take the reins sometime in the future. This morning, he'd said the time had come. Lucas downed the last of his drink. "He told me to pull my head out of my ass and do my duty."

Not a minute too soon, the server refreshed their glasses.

"Which means?"

"Find a wife. Provide an heir."

"Since you haven't mentioned Wynter at all, and the last time I saw you, you announced you planned to pursue her, I'm doing some mental addition and wondering if that's why you look like someone who hasn't slept for a week."

He studied his friend. "I'd say that was a hell of a brilliant deduction. But I'm willing to bet Hope suggested you call me. And because she doesn't want to break any confidentiality agreements, she didn't tell you why. Maybe she even casually asked how I'm doing."

"Bingo." Rafe toasted the reasoning. "Now that we got through that bullshit, what the fuck happened?"

"Bottom line? She's not willing to settle for what I'm offering."

"Which is...?" Rafe prompted.

"Security and comfort."

"Why should she?"

Lucas frowned.

"She's got a great job and a pile of her own money." He shrugged. "To me, it looked as if she was fine before you came along. You have to offer something she wants. Be a little more selfless."

"Come on, man. You remember Ileana." The weeks spent drowning in a drunken stupor. Not that the last days had been much different.

Tuesday after he finally dragged his ass home from work —having failed to lose himself in routine busyness—he'd skipped dinner in favor of a six-pack of beer leftover from his poker night. He'd awakened bleary eyed at three a.m. and stumbled to bed.

The last two nights, he hadn't even put that much effort into it, opting to sleep on the couch without stripping off his clothes.

This morning, the unflappable Edwin had asked Lucas if he was coming down with something and suggested he take the day off.

"You're not seriously comparing Wynter to that lying, cheating bitch, are you?"

"Oh fuck no." She was honest, maybe to the point of

bluntness at times. He couldn't imagine her taking advantage of anyone.

"Ileana cut your heart out and would have happily fed it to you."

She'd done just that.

"So what did Wynter demand?"

"Love."

"But if you didn't care about her, you wouldn't look like shit and smell like a brewery."

Did his friend have to sound so goddamn cheery?

Rafe signaled to the server and ordered dinner for them, pricey steaks. "Figured you'd been living on pizza."

If he bothered with food at all.

When they were alone again, the dark cloud around him closed in even tighter.

"The shit you went through after Ileana betrayed you... how does it compare to what you're going through now?"

This pain was worse. Ileana's behavior had been treacherous, but she'd never loved him. At this moment everything good in him had shattered because he realized he'd crushed Wynter and destroyed her first experience with love. *Fuck.*

Minutes later Rafe had still said nothing. The silence, and the emptiness inside Lucas, was cloying. "I want what you and Hope have."

"What do you think that is?"

"Shared goals. Vision. The way you lean on each other."

"Comes from love, my friend. And it was hard fought. A woman worth having requires effort. Commitment. Sacrifice. You have to take the other's needs into consideration." Rafe pressed his palms together. "It's back to risk assessment. If you were to offer your heart, would it be safe in Wynter's hands? Or would she just trample on it?"

The latter option was so far outside of her personality that Lucas couldn't even conceive of the possibility.

"I'll tell you this, you can't have what you want without risking every damn thing and baring your soul. Go get her back before it's too late."

*"Red."* Rafe hadn't witnessed the pain on her face or heard the sobs that ripped apart her voice. Nor had he seen the tears she'd desperately struggled to hide.

It was already too late.

❦

"It's a man problem, isn't it?" Anna Bella demanded as soon as she climbed out of her car. "I swear to God, you have got to stop having problems with the opposite sex. My body cannot handle all this exercise."

So very grateful for her best friend and her unflappable nature, Wynter cracked a grin, the first one since she'd fled Lucas's office on Tuesday. "I have it on good authority that walking once a week will not kill you."

"Tell that to my knees." She bent to rub them. "Poor things. We'll get you a massage later, so you can feel better."

Wynter rolled her eyes. "Shall we?"

Anna Bella reached back into her car for her hat before huffing out a strained, "If we have to."

Unless she burned off some angst, Wynter might dissolve into a puddle of anguish. Despite her grumbling, the moment she'd answered the phone, Anna Bella had asked only one question: "What time do you want to meet?" Her friend's unconditional support—even though it included participation in an outdoor activity—had instantly decreased Wynter's stress level.

"You know, we could do this at a gym instead."

With skepticism, Wynter frowned. "Really?"

"Yeah." Anna Bella locked her car and fell in step next to Wynter. "Like you could be on a treadmill with some pretty scenery on the screen in front of you. And I'd stand next to you enjoying a cocktail."

At the outrageous suggestion, she cracked the first smile all week. "You can't bring in mixed drinks."

"Well, vodka is clear. Add some water and a powdered energy mix, and voila!"

"You think of everything." She looked over at her friend. "As long as it gets you out of exercising."

"Bonus points for sneaking alcohol into someplace that's supposed to be good for you."

"You're always thinking."

Anna Bella tapped the side of her head. "Gotta use this thing for good as well as evil, you know?"

Unfortunately for Wynter, her brain had been focused more on the bad than the good in recent days. Over and over, she saw the stark expression that had been seared into Lucas's eyes when she used her safe word.

"Is this about His Royal Hindass?"

Wynter laughed. "What did you call him?"

"If he upset you, then I'm pissed off too. By default, you know? We're besties; we roll together. Need help burying the body?"

She wished it were that simple.

"So what happened? I mean, with some hypothetical American prince?"

Wynter provided a synopsis, including the magical BDSM experience.

"He was a good Top?"

Better than that.

"You had a safe word."

"And one for slowing down."

"Excellent. At least I don't have to kick his ass for that. Was he considerate?"

*Definitely so.* Wynter nodded. "And…"

"Talk to me. Tell me all the things."

Talking was cathartic. Last night she'd babysat her nieces. Her stepsister asked how Wynter was doing, but since Lori was stressed and harried with the kids, Wynter said all was well.

Other than Anna Bella, Wynter had no one in her life who would understand what she'd experienced in Galveston and how it was still affecting her. "I hadn't expected the mindfuck to be such a thing. Honestly that was my favorite part. A tone of voice can matter so much."

"For sure." Anna Bella stopped under the shade of a live oak tree.

Wynter didn't object.

"So you'd do it again?"

If it were a perfect world, and Lucas was doing the dominating, she would. But she wasn't willing to trust anyone else. At least not yet.

"When you're ready, if you're ready, just let me know. You can go to the club as my guest."

"Maybe in the future."

"So the BDSM was good?"

"Yes." She shifted beneath the power of Anna Bella's scrutiny. Wynter decided her friend was right. The sun was uncomfortably hot.

"So tell me again why we're having trouble with the prince."

"The computer found him a woman who is a hundred percent match. The perfect wife."

"That's it." Anna Bella folded her arms. "I need a fucking shovel. Some hot woman shows up and he dumps you?"

"*No!*" She shook her head. "That's not what happened."

"Talk fast because I feel like someone needs his royal ass kicked."

"He told me he's still interested in me."

"Oh. Oh. So you dumped him?"

From his perspective, no doubt she had. "There's only one thing I want from a relationship."

Anna Bella, much more practical than Wynter, waved her fingers in the air, simulating butterflies flitting about. "Starry-eyed love."

"Yeah."

"Which his cold heart ain't capable of?"

For the first time Wynter understood why Lucas had marked his heart as off-limits. Loving and losing was the most soul-crushing thing she'd ever endured. "I got out while I could still save myself." And now she planned to lock away her own heart so she didn't go through this ever again.

Anna Bella wrapped her arm around Wynter's shoulders. "I knew the moment you called that it was a world-class emergency, so I booked us appointments at the spa."

"What?" She blinked. "Are you serious? I can't go to the spa. I've been working out. And I need a shower."

"They have them. And an entire shop filled with workout clothes. Yoga pants and such. You'll love it." Anna Bella turned them in the direction of the cars. "Girl, we are so gonna go and wash that man right out of your hair."

# CHAPTER NINE

Wynter's office phone buzzed from Miriam's extension. "Your eleven a.m. appointment is here."

With a frown, Wynter clicked her mouse to toggle from the client portal to her calendar program. There was nothing marked on it.

After her break-up with Lucas, he had ended his contract with Prestige, and Hope had swamped her with work, maybe realizing it was the one thing holding Wynter together. She'd even started helping the part-timers vet the people who would be invited to the mixers. The more she learned about the business the better.

Surely she wasn't so busy that she'd forgotten to note an appointment. "Who is it?"

"A new client. Hope escorted him to the conference room."

"Thanks. I'll be right there." After finger-combing her hair, Wynter stood and smoothed the front of her dress. Then she walked toward the reception area.

A woman stood there, placing an enormous food delivery

box on Miriam's table. The thing was so big that Miriam couldn't see over the top.

"Who is it from?" Wynter asked the delivery person.

"La Patisserie."

"The confectionery at the Sterling Uptown?"

"Cleared out our entire pastry case."

"Wow. Who placed the order?"

She checked the receipt. "It's for Wynter Ferguson."

"For…?" Wynter blinked.

"That's her." Miriam stood and pointed to Wynter.

"Hope you enjoy!" She turned to leave.

"Wait! I need to give you a tip."

"It's already handled."

"Do you know anything about this?" Wynter asked Miriam.

"I'm as confused as you are."

Before she could remove it from the front desk, another person walked in, laden with trays of coffee—some large, some small. All the cups had tickets with names on them, one for each associate.

"Is it someone's birthday?" Wynter asked, signing the receipt. "Or maybe Hope's trying to surprise us?" After all, she'd just signed three new clients.

Miriam shrugged. "What are we going to do with this stuff?"

"Put it in the conference room until we figure it out?" She picked up a tray and headed that direction.

She opened the door, and a balloon floated out. Then, before she even crossed the threshold, the scent of fresh-cut flowers assailed her.

Inside, she froze.

Among a thousand or so helium and regular balloons, and dozens of bouquets, stood Lucas and Hope.

"I…" Her knees threatened to buckle, and the tray of

drinks started to dip. Frantically she adjusted her grip and straightened her body before every coffee toppled to the floor. "What…"

She struggled to take everything in.

Lucas, though heart-stoppingly handsome, had lost some weight. The last time she'd seen him, she'd noted tiny lines etched beside his steel-gray eyes. They were still there, but the grooves were deeper. From stress? Or something else.

Despite all of her internal pep talks about how she needed to get over him, emotion flooded her. Her mind recognized how dangerous he was. Her traitorous heart knew what it wanted.

"I don't want to leave you alone with Lucas, unless you're okay with it." Hope came over to take the tray from Wynter's hands.

To her, it seemed the world had stood still, grinding time to a halt, but in reality only a second or two had passed.

"Tell Hope it's okay." His voice wasn't commanding, it was hoarse with emotion.

*No.* "I…"

Hope scowled at Lucas before looking back at Wynter with compassion. "I will escort him out right this moment if that's what you want."

"Five minutes. That's all I need. The door can stay open, so that you know you're safe."

At that moment, Tony walked past, and he sneezed ferociously.

"He's allergic to most flowers," Hope explained. "We found out the hard way."

Wynter nodded to Lucas. "You can have five minutes."

"Thank you."

"I'll be waiting in the reception area." Hope excused herself.

Then they were alone, and the room seemed to shrink.

"I've missed you."

"Don't." She held up a hand. "Please." Her voice cracked, revealing the upset she desperately wanted to hide. "Why are you here?"

"To tell you I'm a fucking idiot."

Pressing her hand to her heart, she couldn't help a small smile. "We agree on something."

"You offered me a gift—your love. And I didn't cherish it like I should have."

"The clock is ticking." She wasn't sure how to survive the next three and a half minutes. "And I need to get back to work."

He raked a hand through his hair, mussing it in a way that reminded her of their time at the hotel and how informal and comfortable they'd once been together.

"I'm here to apologize, but that's not all."

"If you hoped I'd fall into your arms because of the coffee, balloons—"

"And pastries, flowers, all your favorite things."

"Nice try. But no. It's not working. Because of you, my heart is also hardened. I let you in once. And that was too many times."

"I've had plenty of time to think about what matters." He lifted a hand as if to touch her face, but when she took another step back, he dropped it to his side. "About you. About us."

"There is no *us,* thanks to you."

"There could be."

"No." She was resolute.

"Wynter…" His voice broke. "I'm here, opening my heart, begging your forgiveness."

She wanted nothing more than to wave a magic wand and create her perfect life. But that wasn't possible. "I have to admit that I blame myself more than you. Right from the start, you were honest." She shook her head. "It was even on your intake form. That I fell for you is on me. In the future, I will do much better at listening when people tell me who they are."

"Who I was."

"Your time is up, Lucas. If you'll excuse me…?"

"Wynter. I love you."

Unadulterated shock riveted her in place. Those were the words she ached to hear, that she'd dreamed of.

"It took you walking away for me to recognize the truth." He winced. "And Rafe kicking my ass for me to realize what a total fool I had been. You offered everything you had, and I was locked in my past, thinking only about myself. I acted from fear. Now I prefer to look at the future, one filled with happiness, children, a partnership that grows and deepens through the years. Can you forgive me?"

His words were too, too much to take in.

"If you can, I will spend the rest of my life making up for my mistakes. I want to show you my love every day. You demanded more from me than anyone else ever has, and I'm glad you did. You've made me a better, more humble man."

He lowered himself to one knee and pulled out an exquisite diamond ring. "Wynter. I love you. Will you marry me?"

Oh God. This moment, with this man, was everything she'd dreamed. "I…"

"We don't have to get married right away, unless you want to. But if you want to be sure you can trust it, us, I'll be patient. But let me put a ring on your finger as a symbol of my love and never-ending commitment to us."

Words lodged around the lump of emotion in her throat. Tears spilled from her eyes.

"I'm terrorized with fear here." He tried to smile, but it didn't reach his eyes. "Show me some mercy."

"Yes." Her entire body shook from the force of the walls crumbling from around her heart.

With a grip that was equal parts firm and tender, he took her hand and slid the exquisite diamond ring into place. The gem winked in the lighting and reflected the bright pink from one of the balloons. "It's stunning."

His kiss was tempting, rich with promise. Then he groaned and kissed her deeper, long and slow.

When he ended it, he stared into her eyes forever. "This is what happiness looks like. And I want to memorize every detail."

She linked her arms around his neck and leaned against him. He responded, hugging her tight.

"I love you, Lucas. And I fell for you from the moment you beckoned me over. As if instinctively I knew you were the one for me."

"Every time I think I couldn't adore you more, I fall a little deeper. I will never again let you go."

He'd been vulnerable, and how could she be any less so? "I'm not sure I could bear it."

Against her belly, his cock stirred. "I need to get you home."

She wanted nothing more. "But...I can't. I have to work."

"I'll deal with your boss. After all, she'll be getting a big fat check from me today."

"Wait. We didn't match you." She frowned.

"Hope told me if I married you, I was paying the fee. I think she was trying to discourage me from pursuing you." He grinned. "It didn't work."

He took her hand as they walked down the hallway. No one was in their offices. Instead, the team had gathered in the reception area, and they broke into applause when they entered.

"Congratulations!" Skyler called.

Amidst squeals of excitement, Wynter was swept into hugs, and the ladies oohed and aahed over her ring as they peppered questions she didn't have answers to.

The moment, shared with her coworkers, was perfect.

"My bride-to-be is taking the rest of the day off."

Hope grinned. "Of course. I doubt she'd get much work done if she stayed." Then she looked at Wynter. "You've got plenty of accrued time off, so you're welcome to take a few days if you'd like."

"Are you sure?"

"Absolutely. This is a moment to celebrate."

Lucas swept her off her feet, and Tony opened the door while Skyler dove into the pastry delivery box.

The sounds of cheers followed them all the way to the elevator.

Once they were inside and the doors slid closed, he finally set her down, only to pin her against the side wall for his searing, demanding kiss.

"I'm not sure I can wait to get you home."

"Well, there are cameras everywhere, including the parking garage."

"Not that I care about my reputation, but I do care about yours."

Because it was closer, they went to her house where he carried her inside and straight through to the bedroom.

"We've got some lost time to make up for, my future bride."

"Do you know where you'd like to start?"

"Why, Ms. Ferguson, I do believe I have an idea or two." With a wicked grin, he captured her dress, then swept it up and off.

She kept her gaze focused on him as she shimmied her panties down her thighs. Then she stepped out of them. "Maybe you should show me. Sir."

"I believe I will, and it will be my pleasure to show you for the rest of our lives."

⌒

"And the prince and princess lived happily ever after." Lucas closed the book and leaned forward to slide it onto the coffee table.

From where she lounged against the wall of her stepsister's living room, Wynter smiled. When Lori discovered Wynter and Lucas wanted to have children, she suggested he get in some weekly practice.

Leaving her speechless, he'd agreed. Now, every Tuesday, they picked up pizza and babysat her nieces. Generally they played—and Lucas had attended several pretend tea parties —colored, or watched a fun television show.

But their favorite part was when he read them a bedtime story. And this week, they'd talked him into a second book.

Before the girls could demand another, which would keep them up way past their bedtime, Wynter scooped the youngest off the couch. Growling like a bear, Lucas picked up the four-year-old.

After tucking the girls in and fetching them both a drink of water, Lucas and Wynter returned to the living room to clean up the tornado of toys strewn across the floor.

Lucas shook his head. "This place was immaculate when we got here."

"It's mind boggling how fast they can pull it all out." And exhaust the adults in the process.

Instead of relaxing on the couch, he gathered a bunch of

toys and placed them in the carefully labeled boxes while she cleaned up the kitchen.

Babysitting each week had reassured her that getting engaged had been the right decision. Lucas was open, relaxed with the kids, and his laughter eased the stress lines from his face.

They had just snuggled together on the couch when Lori returned.

"I can't thank you two enough." Mascara was gently smudged beneath her eyes from her shift as an ER nurse. "You're a godsend. No one else cleans up after them." Then she wrinkled her nose. "Do I smell pizza?"

"Lucas saved you a piece."

"Thank you. I didn't have lunch." She yawned, which Wynter took as their cue to leave.

City traffic was light as they made their way back to his spacious high-rise condo. Slowly she'd been moving over some of her personal belongings, with an eye to putting her townhome on the market soon. He was ready to have her in and settled.

They were in the bathroom together, and she was filling the tub with hot water when dramatic music blasted from his watch.

*A genius is trying to reach you.*

Wynter laughed. "Julien Bonds?"

A hologram of Bonds floated on top of the watch, and he was silhouetted in spotlights. "Thank you, Rutherford Consulting. You'll look good on the red carpet. Buy a tuxedo. Toodles!"

The image winked out.

"You decided to invest?"

"Not sure why." He shrugged. "I could lose every penny."

"Trust yourself." She turned off the water and sank into

the tub. "Even if it fails, you have plenty of other investments that are doing well?"

"And if we lose everything?"

It was still a fear, but not as prevalent as it once was. "We'll start over." As she told him, she'd be happy even with a secondhand car and a small apartment as long as they were together.

"Not sure what I did to deserve you."

"Took a risk."

They chatted for a few more minutes. Then his eyes darkened as he offered a hand to help her out. "Did you know that spanks sting more when the skin is wet?"

"I'll be the judge of that, Sir."

He grinned as if to say, *"Challenge accepted."*

"Make sure your hands and feet are dry, and then place your palms on the wall."

The dominance edging his tone heated her blood.

"Tonight, I'm not going to warm you up first. I want you to feel this."

She recalled a time that would have terrified her. But curiosity accompanied experience. Most evenings they indulged in at least an abbreviated BDSM scene, with longer ones on the weekends. For her it was as much about connection as well as the stress relief.

Lucas came up behind her, flattened her body against the wall, his cock surging against her, demanding satisfaction. After kissing her, he gently sank his teeth into her shoulder, leaving her dizzy with desire.

After he stepped back, she turned her head in time to see him release his belt buckle. Then he pulled the leather free of its straps.

Pressing her lips together against her sudden nerves, she took a shallow breath.

He gave her three of his best stripes. On dry skin, his belt burned, but now that she was wet, the sensation rocked her.

Fighting back hiccupping sobs, she dropped her forehead onto her arms.

"My precious little one."

Small droplets of water still clung to parts of her body when he led her to the bedroom and cuffed her hands behind her back. Then he slid lightweight tweezer clamps onto her nipples. "You're driving me wild, Sir."

He studied her carefully. "That doesn't sound like a safe word."

"No, Sir. It's not." In fact, her pussy was aching, and she was slick from the desire for his possession.

After undressing and sheathing himself with a condom, he sat on the chair. "Are you ready to come, Wynter?"

Desperately she nodded.

"Work for it." He lowered her onto his cock.

Her ass stinging, her nipples burning, hands imprisoned so that she was unable to hold him, she rode him hard, but she couldn't quite reach the orgasm she craved.

With a wicked gleam in his eyes, he tightened the clamps, and when she whimpered, he captured the sound with his mouth.

In his dominant way, he took over, holding her waist, lifting and lowering her.

"Come for me, little one."

Crying out from the onslaught of pleasure, she came.

It was only after she was completely satisfied that he sought his own orgasm.

With gentle motions, he unfastened her, then held her cradled against his chest.

Happier than she'd ever been, she remained there, feeling the reassuring beat of his heart. "It just keeps getting better."

"And it's only the beginning."

◊ ◊ ◊ ◊ ◊

Thank you for reading Ruthless Billionaire. I've been thinking about Lucas for years. In fact, I was so enthralled with him that I drafted the opening pages about eighteen months ago. But it took me a long time to really get to know him and figure out what event had hurt him so bad that he refused to offer his heart ever again.

I hope you love him as much as I do.

If you like the intriguing and powerful Titans, I invite you to discover His to Claim. It's the first book in the bingeable Titans The Quarter series, set in New Orleans. All the heroes are ultra-dominant and fabulously sexy.

Hannah had only agreed to a weekend together. Now Mason—the overwhelming billionaire—is demanding her heart forever.

**DISCOVER HIS TO CLAIM**

Don't miss out on special bonus reads and all the Scanda-licious news about upcoming releases and special announcements.

Become a VIP newsletter subscriber today!

What can be better than two ultra-delicious alpha Domi-nants? How about *two* ultra-delicious alpha Dominants?

They are billionaires accustomed to getting what they want —and they will stop at nothing to claim her.

★★★★★ "This is a glorious MFM menage, with two dominants and our inexperienced sub." ~Amazon Reviewer

**DISCOVER THEIRS TO HOLD**

Turn the page for an exciting excerpt from **HIS TO CLAIM**

# HIS TO CLAIM

## CHAPTER ONE

There were a hell of a lot better ways Mason could be spending his Friday night. Watching a documentary on television, for example. Doing woodwork in his shop. Putting together ideas for his upcoming pitch to a home and garden network for a renovation show.

Instead, not looking forward to the evening, Mason pushed through the door that led from the stairs to the reception area of the Quarter, New Orleans' most exclusive BDSM club.

Because of the large number of guests arriving for tonight's charity slave auction, Aviana, the owner, was helping the receptionist check people in. When she spotted him, she smiled. A moment later, she excused herself and rounded the podium to greet him. "Mason!"

"Milady." He raised her hand to his lips. "Radiant, as always."

Tonight, the tall, willowy woman looked fierce, every bit the Mistress she was. Her boots snuggled her thighs, and the heels sent her soaring past six feet tall. Her two-piece outfit was sensational. The skirt and cropped jacket-type top were brown leather armor and adorned with hundreds of metal pyramid spikes. Her long hair was piled on top of her head, and silver pins were stabbed into it, making sure none of the strands dared attempt an escape.

"You look dashing," she said, smoothing one of his lapels.

"It's rented."

"Your secret is safe with me."

It wasn't a secret. Mason spent his days in blue jeans, well-worn boots, and T-shirts as he visited his job sites. When he had the chance, he swung the hammer himself.

"I didn't expect to see you."

"You…" He cleared his throat. *Coerced.* "Convinced me."

She smiled with obvious triumph.

To be fair, he owed her the show of support. They both served on the board of a charity his father had started, rehabilitating homes for the city's elderly population. And once a year, Aviana hosted a fundraiser that helped make their work possible. He'd skipped last year's event, and she'd made a point of mentioning that fact at each of their monthly meetings ever since.

Still, this was the last place he wanted to be. He preferred to visit the Quarter on those rare occasions when he desired the connection with a submissive.

"Program?" Aviana offered, taking one of the folded pieces of paper from the top of the podium.

He shook his head. "That won't be necessary. Thanks." Mason had no intention of bidding on any of the women participating in the slave auction.

"Who knows? Perhaps you might be tempted."

To spend an entire weekend with a woman he'd purchased? Not likely. It had been more than two years since he'd invited anyone to share his bed. He checked his watch. "What time can I escape?"

"The festivities should end around midnight."

"Drinks being served?"

"The bar is closed until the auction ends."

He generally appreciated her rules. Right now? Not so much. The next few hours would be much easier with a nice bourbon.

A crowd entered the foyer, filling the space with laughter.

"We'll catch up later?" she suggested. "Perhaps lunch within the next couple of weeks?"

"As long as it's friendly, with no written agenda."

"Of course."

He eyed her suspiciously, unsure whether she was telling the truth.

Aviana turned away, then stopped to look back over her shoulder. "I'm glad you came."

He gave her a half smile. It was the best he could manage. Until he picked up the tux a few hours ago, he hadn't been sure he'd actually attend.

Mason pushed through the frosted-glass door leading to the dungeon that was filled with loud, thumping music, no doubt meant to excite the crowd.

The first thing he noticed was Aviana's throne, placed on a raised dais off to one side where she could lord over the event.

All the usual play equipment had been removed from the area. The Saint Andrew's crosses were lined up against the walls, with spanking benches placed in front of them.

A stage had been erected at the far end of the room. Never one to do things by half measures, Aviana had hired lighting and camera crews and had positioned two large screens at angles so that all attendees would have a good view.

Comfortable padded chairs had been arranged in precise rows for the bidders and gawkers who'd paid Aviana's exorbitant admission fee. He knew exactly how much it was, since she'd billed his ticket to the credit card the club kept on file for his incidental expenses.

Numerous gilded cages hung from the ceiling, all containing at least one person, several containing two. The entertainers moved in time to the music, some holding on to a wire in the top, others grabbing the bars, a few sliding up and down. The atmosphere seethed with energy.

For twenty minutes, he talked to a few people he knew and thanked them for attending and supporting the charity.

Suddenly the lights dimmed. Music shut off, and as if on cue, performers froze in place in their cages.

"Welcome to the Quarter!" The words reverberated through the dungeon, loud and commanding.

On the stage, a flash exploded, and a stunning couple appeared near the edge. They were tall, exceedingly thin, and they looked so much alike he guessed they were twins, though one appeared to be female, the other male.

They were dressed identically in stark-white pantsuits. Each had enormous eyes, with long, feathery lashes. Stunningly, they also sported dark hair, cut in a long bob, accented by angular bangs. Aviana was providing her guests with a spectacle. Despite himself, Mason was intrigued.

The twins clapped in unison, then spoke as one. "Ladies and gentlemen, your seats, please."

Dungeon monitors urged attendees toward the chairs. Mason remained where he was, back pressed against the wall. Tore, Aviana's massive bearded chief dungeon monitor, nodded his permission to allow Mason to stay where he was.

As soon as everyone was in place, the twins spoke again. "Please rise for Mistress Aviana."

The doors were thrown open, and Aviana stalked into the room. Two beautiful male submissives trailed behind her, their leashes attached to her epaulets.

She made her way down the center aisle. With each step,

the gold in her outfit shimmered beneath the spotlights that were turned on her. When she neared the front of the room, Tore fell in step next to her, then offered his hand as she climbed onto her dais.

After waving to acknowledge her adoring crowd, she took her seat on the throne. It had been commissioned years before by an admiring sub, and Aviana's likeness was carved into the top. The rounded arm ends were custom-made from a plaster cast of her grip. As befitting her stature, the upholstery was the finest maroon-colored velvet. It had been crafted with hooks in strategic places where she could attach a slave or submissive.

Once her subs were settled, curled at her feet and chained in place, the twins invited the audience to return to their chairs.

Aviana didn't put on many displays of her dominance, but when she did, the power of her command was as impressive as hell. His gaze strayed to the men at her feet.

At one time, he'd had a submissive who showed him the same kind of deference. But behaving well during a scene hadn't meant a flying fuck outside of it. When she finally left him—at the worst possible time—part of him had been relieved. Since then, he'd avoided personal entanglements.

Until this moment, he hadn't missed having a sub.

Maybe Aviana had been right to encourage him to visit the Quarter more often.

The twins introduced the evening's emcee, Jaxon Mills, a renowned—and at times polarizing—internet marketing superstar. The man had in excess of a million followers on his social media platforms, people who hung on his every video and podcast. He'd started giving speeches to rapt audiences, and since his recent marriage, he'd evidently stepped up his volunteer work as well.

A spotlight hit Jax as he all but leaped onto the stage. He

pointed a finger, then swept it wide, indicating everyone in the crowd. "Get your checkbooks out and your credit cards ready. We have the world's most stunning subs available for you tonight. And it's all for a good cause. You've heard of Reclamation, a charity that benefits seniors living in our great city." On the screens, a video started, showing volunteers scraping paint, hammering shingles into place, installing windows, working on plumbing, replacing furniture and appliances. Everyone was dressed in T-shirts bearing the charity's logo. Volunteers were dirty, sweaty, but smiling, often pictured with the residents they were helping.

Surprising Mason, several of the images included a picture of him.

Without losing a beat, Jaxon continued. "This is what your contribution does. As you know, the need in our community is great. Because of your abundant contributions, last year we restored more than two hundred homes. If you were one of the heroes who made that possible, thank you." He pushed his palms together and bowed. "But let's be honest, shall we?" His voice was low and intimate.

The man's charisma had the room spellbound.

"You know damn good and well that you're fortunate sons of bitches. You can do a fuckpile more than you do. You can dig deeper. If you don't help out tonight, you're a loser, and I'm calling you out on it. We're here for a purpose, and that isn't just to leer at some gorgeous humans. It's to leer *and* make our city proud."

"Hear, hear!" a woman called out.

The video ended, and he stood there in a shimmering pool of light.

When the raucous clapping ended, Jax reached inside his tuxedo jacket, pulled out his wallet, and extracted a check. "Can I get a close-up, please?" Jax held up the piece of paper.

The audience gasped, and Mason nodded approvingly. A

hundred grand. Not a bad way to start the evening. There was a stunning amount of good they could do with that kind of money.

"I have a confession." Jaxon folded the check and used a thumbnail to make the crease sharp. "I'd budgeted fifty thousand for this event. But my wife watched this video. After seeing it, she volunteered for the charity."

A spotlight found a woman who was at the front of the room. She wore a long gold gown, formfitting and glittering with sequins.

"In case you don't know, this is my wife, Willow Mills."

People cheered for her, and Mason knew, firsthand, it was deserved. Despite being a submissive, she was next to her husband, and he credited her with helping him become a better man.

"Tell them what you said to me, honey."

"I told *you* not to be a cheapskate"—a close-up image of her face was being projected on the screen, and her eyes danced with laughter that showed the love between them—"Sir."

The crowd exploded with laughter and more applause.

"All right, all right!" He grinned. When the attendees settled again, he went on. "So I'm passing along her words. Don't be a damn cheapskate. Our seniors have given so much over the years. It's time to give back. And hey, if you're not bidding, or you miss out on your favorite slave, you aren't off the hook."

More hoots and cheers greeted his words.

"There are silent auction items in the bar and reception areas. I know you want to hear some of the highlights. How about a week on a private island in the Caribbean? Griffin Lahey has made the donation, and your stay there includes a chef and an outdoor massage for two." Images scrolled across the screens, of a couple snorkeling among tiny bright-colored fish, then lounging on chairs beneath an umbrella, a cocktail in hand. A sunset was shown next, with kayaks seemingly being rowed out toward it.

How long had it been since Mason had taken a vacation? *Shit*. He dragged his hand through his hair. Not since his dad had passed. The year before that, Mason had been swamped with trying to keep the business running by himself. Maybe that explained his soul-deep exhaustion.

"If that's not your style, how about a high-roller weekend at the Royal Sterling Hotel in Las Vegas?" The resort was pictured, soaring from the Strip with its glass sparkling against the desert sun.

Though Mason wasn't a gambler, the restaurants were legendary, and the pool was the stuff of fantasies. He could sleep there for a week. *Jesus.* He really did need to get away.

"Perhaps you'd like to fall in love with New York this autumn with a package that includes tickets to the hottest performances"—the pictures showed Broadway, then Grand Central Station—"a horse-drawn carriage ride through Central Park, and three nights and unlimited possibilities in the penthouse suite at Le Noble."

Even though he had no one to invite along, Mason was tempted to bid on every damn one of the escapes.

"We have something for every taste. How about a signed giclée by Flahey?"

A few people gasped at the sight of the bold colors and staggering lines slashed across the canvas. Mason knew the artist was well respected. He just didn't understand why. The image was supposed to be of a rock star. If he squinted and turned his head to the side, he could make out a guitar. Maybe. Still, the man commanded a fortune from collectors. The cynic in Mason would definitely prefer that money go to Reclamation.

"If you don't win a weekend with one of the Quarter's

amazing subs or one of our spectacular prizes, we'll still accept your more than generous contribution at the end of the evening. There will be boxes throughout the space, at the coat check, at the exit, and a bunch at the bar. Oh, and one last thing—free drinks for anyone who donates more than five grand." He paused for dramatic effect. "I hope you were prepared for me giving away your booze, Mistress Aviana!"

The camera flashed to her. She gave a half smile and a very regal nod.

"Ah, and finally, anyone who donates over ten thousand dollars will get an exclusive half-day consultation with me."

That was reportedly worth a lot more than ten grand. Jax was gifted at studying a business, branding it, focusing on its strengths, and positioning it for success.

"And if you don't contribute something, your name is going on my shitlist."

His statement was met with laughter—some genuine, some nervous.

"In case this is your first auction, I'll give you a little background on how the evening will proceed. We have a total of fifteen slaves. Yes, fifteen gorgeous, well-behaved individuals"—he looked directly into the camera—"who want to spend the weekend with *you.*"

"Get on with it!" someone shouted.

"They will be presented for your inspection in groups of five. After all the introductions have been made, we will have a brief intermission, and then the bidding will start. Now... who's ready to begin?"

The dungeon plunged into darkness. Moments later, strategic lights hit the stage and the overhead cages with their writhing occupants. Cheers rocked the room, and music again blasted through the air, a thumping, arousing sound that penetrated even Mason's jaded senses.

Behind Jaxon, a black curtain parted to reveal a large

rectangular acrylic platform with two steps leading up to it. There were other round see-through pedestals fanned out in a semicircle.

Jax moved to one side, and Tore strode onto the stage. As usual, he wore a vest. Tonight, however, instead of the customary one with fleur-de-lis, this was crafted from the same brown leather as Mistress Aviana's, and it hung open to show off his honed abs.

Over his shoulder was a long, thick chain, with the first five volunteer slaves attached to it. The group was eclectic. Tall and short. Male and female. Of various ages and ethnicities. Men wore only a scrap of stark-white material, not much more than a pouch that left little to the imagination. The women were dressed in string bikinis beneath sheer sarongs.

The twins floated onto the stage. Together, they unclipped the first slave from the chain and assisted her onto one of the platforms. The camera followed each of her flawless moves.

They repeated the process for each participant. When they were finished, they stepped aside while the camera panned the semicircle. Most of the slaves were relaxed, and one of the men was flexing his biceps, trying to draw attention.

"There you are!" Jaxon called. "It's going to be an extraordinary night!"

Adrenaline fired through the room in the form of claps and appreciative whistles. As much as Mason wanted to be immune, he wasn't. It was a hell of a spectacle.

"Ladies and gentlemen, I present slave number one," Jaxon said when the audience settled down.

The twins helped the first sub from her platform and escorted her to the front of the stage where she stood in the spotlight.

She lowered her gaze, then gave a quick peep through her lashes. It was seductive. Judging by the way one member of the audience sucked in a sharp breath, it was also effective.

"Fiona is looking for a top who is firm but fair. And fortunately for you, she's happy to be won by either a man or a woman." He went on to list her limits and then asked her to turn around so the bidders could study her from every angle. "The minimum bid will be five thousand dollars."

Several people used lights from their cell phones to scribble notes into the margins of their programs. The woman, as beautiful and obviously well trained as she was, didn't stir Mason.

After she'd turned around and presented herself in a variety of poses, the twins returned her to Tore, then escorted the second slave, a man, to the spotlight.

The process was repeated until all the slaves had been introduced. Once they were led away, the next set was brought on. Mason checked his watch. As he'd tried to tell Aviana, this wasn't his kind of event. He either came to scene or he stayed away.

After an interminable amount of time, Tore led the final group in for viewing.

And the woman who was second in line snared his interest.

She was at least half a foot shorter than he was, with impossibly large, wide-open eyes, and brunette hair that tumbled over her shoulders. The gauzy film that covered her couldn't disguise her small, beautiful figure. The building's air-conditioning hardened her nipples. To him, she was a tiny wisp of feminine perfection.

Repeating the same process as with the other participants, the twins unclipped her from Tore's chain. As she walked toward her acrylic platform, she missed a step and stumbled slightly. The twins reached for her upper arms to steady her. All the other slaves had appeared to be veterans and enjoying themselves, but her actions betrayed her as a novice.

Mason was torn, his dominant urges stirred. Part of him wanted to protect her. The other, more primal part of his nature urged him to make her his.

What the fuck was wrong with him?

He wasn't given to wild fantasies. Or, maybe he had been, once upon a time. But that had been before Deborah.

The slave gave a quick smile of gratitude before stepping up onto her display platform.

The twins moved aside, and the spotlight moved on to the next contestant. But he looked toward the shadowed part of the stage to watch number twelve. Her shoulders shook, and she curled one hand around the small collar she wore.

He was consumed with a need to know more about her. Why the hell hadn't he accepted one of the programs?

Mason checked his watch again, but for a different reason this time. He was anxious for the pomp and circumstance to be over with so he could have a better look at her.

After the other subs were in place, the first sub was brought forward. His impatience soared. He was interested in only one woman.

Finally, the twins led her to the front of the stage where she stood next to Jax. Her image was projected onto the big screens, making her larger than life. Confounding him, she kept her head lowered, shading her expression.

"Hannah joins us this weekend from Austin, Texas."

When she wobbled a little, Jaxon steadied her, and she grabbed on to him.

Even though he covered his mic to ask if she was all right, the words whispered through the dungeon. "Bend your knees a little. It will help."

She nodded and did what he said.

"Do you want to continue?"

She dropped her hand to her side and nodded several times. "Just nerves."

After Jax studied her for a few seconds, he continued. "Hannah prefers a male Dom who is patient but unyielding. Her limits list includes canes, humiliation, isolation, being shared."

Suited Mason fine. After all, he intended to keep her for himself.

**CONTINUE READING HIS TO CLAIM**

# ABOUT THE AUTHOR

I invite you to be the very first to know all the news by subscribing to my very special **VIP Reader newsletter**! You'll find exclusive excerpts, bonus reads, and insider information.

https://www.sierracartwright.com/subscribe

For tons of fun and to join with other awesome people like you, join my Facebook reader group: **Sierra's Super Stars**

https://www.facebook.com/groups/SierrasSuperStars

And for a current booklist, please visit my **website**.
http://www.sierracartwright.com

USA Today bestselling author Sierra Cartwright was born in England, and she spent her early childhood traipsing through castles and dreaming of happily-ever afters. She has two wonderful kids and four amazing grand-kitties. She now calls Galveston, Texas home and loves to connect with her readers. Please do drop her a note.

# ALSO BY SIERRA CARTWRIGHT

**Titans**

Sexiest Billionaire

Billionaire's Matchmaker

Billionaire's Christmas

Determined Billionaire

Scandalous Billionaire

Ruthless Billionaire

**Titans Quarter**

His to Claim

His to Love

His to Cherish

**Titans Sin City**

Hard Hand

Slow Burn

All-In

**Titans Captivated**

Theirs to Hold

Theirs to Love

*Titans Series*

Titans Billionaires: Firsts

Titans Billionaires: Volume 1

*Hawkeye Series*

Here for Me: Volume One

Beg For Me: Volume Two

*Titans Quarter Series*

Billionaires' Quarter

*Titans Sin City Series*

Risking It All

Printed in Great Britain
by Amazon

21916226R00106